About t ....u.

Now retired and living in Spain, Frank Aulton is an ex-coal miner and a qualified dog trainer. He is the founder of Aldridge Dog Training Club, which is still going strong after 42 years.
He was told when he was at mining college that one day he would write a book. (He is a late starter!)

In memory of Pe-pe

My wife and I are also qualified canine beauticians and we had our own poodle parlour in the 1970s. This story is based on a toy poodle I used to collect. She would not travel in the carrying basket. She was always sick. Neither would she travel on the passenger seat. She always sat on my lap with her paws on the steering wheel. She had the most lovable character and I still think of her after all these years. I dedicate this book to her memory.

Frank Aulton

THE ADVENTURES OF PO-PO

AUSTIN MACAULEY
PUBLISHERS LTD.

A CIP catalogue record for this title is available from the British Library.

ISBN 978 1 78455 577 1 (Paperback)
ISBN 978 1 78455 578 8 (Hardback)

www.austinmacauley.com

First Published (2015)
Austin Macauley Publishers Ltd.
25 Canada Square
Canary Wharf
London
E14 5LB

Printed and bound in Great Britain

Acknowledgments

Thanks to Pam and Mark for help with computer work.

Chapter 1

I remember my first encounter with the human beings. I couldn't have been very old because I was still living with my parents and my two sisters. We lived in a large pen surrounded by a high wooden fence. I was very busy digging a hole in the soft earth, I wasn't very big and the soil kept falling back in as I scraped away with my paws. I called to my sisters to come and help me but they were too busy wrestling with each other; Mother and Father lay side by side, watching them. My sisters must have heard the humans approaching because they scurried past me and tried to hide behind my parents.

Hearing voices, I looked up. There were three of them leaning on the fence looking down at us. I watched my father stand up and bare his teeth at them. I could hear mother whimpering softly to herself. Sensing something was wrong I gave a little yap. I looked at my father, wondering what he was going to do next. Mother was talking to him but I couldn't hear what she was saying though she tried hard to keep her voice to a whisper.

"It's no use Pepe," she said, looking at father, "they're going to take one of our babies."

My heart leapt as she began to whimper again. I stood my ground, fixing my eyes on the humans as they talked amongst themselves. Giving a defiant yap I crouched into position ready to spring into action at my father's command. I think that must have been my biggest mistake of my life.

The man bent over and scooped me up in his big hands, I saw father take a step forward but it was too late, I felt myself being carried away. The frantic barking of my parents died away as they carried me into the house. That was the last time I ever saw my family. Another woman joined them in the room.

"I see you have picked one, then" she said, reaching out for me.

I began to tremble, not knowing what was going on. All I knew was that they had taken me away from my home. I became very frightened. The woman started brushing my coat, trying to clean me up a bit. I struggled and nipped at her but my teeth had no effect on the tough skin.

"I think you have made a good choice," said the woman, handing me back to the man. The rest of the humans gathered round and began poking their fingers at me, so I curled my lips back in defiance. Suddenly I realised that they weren't trying to hurt me; they were just tickling me. I relaxed a little, feeling very tired. "Oh she's going to sleep," I heard the little girl say as they carried me out of the house. "Can I carry her, Daddy'?"

I felt myself being passed over to the little girl. I must have fallen asleep because when I opened my eyes I could hear a low humming noise. The gentle rocking of whatever we were in lulled me back into a deep slumber.

Opening my eyes once more I felt myself being jostled about as the young girl struggled to get out of the container. I looked back at the strange thing. I discovered later that they referred to it as "the car". Once again I was being carried into a house; it was not the same one as I had been in before, it was much nicer. The girl put me down on the floor as the man closed the door. Feeling an urgent need coming on I stooped down and relieved myself. Apparently the humans weren't very pleased at this. Immediately I was scooped up and hurriedly taken outside. Placing me on the grass the little girl began shouting at me. I didn't know what I had done wrong but whatever it was they were not amused. I was beginning to feel hungry by now the girl must have read my mind for she took me back into the house and put a saucer of milk in front of me. I lapped it up quickly as they looked on. I was still confused; I had no idea where I was or what they were going to do with me. The woman placed another saucer in front of me with some meat on it. I ate away ravenously, much to their amusement. Feeling much better, I began to wander around the house. The humans watched every movement I made; it was quite obvious they didn't trust me. The girl disappeared briefly, returning with a small white object, which she rolled in front of me. I watched fascinated as the round thing bounced about on the floor. I was curiously aroused, I chased after it; this seemed to amuse them as they burst into laughter. I began to feel more relaxed as the little girl played with me. Suddenly my stomach felt as if it was on fire. I opened my mouth as the contents erupted, the burning in my throat brought tears to my eyes.

"She's being sick," the girl cried out.

The humans came to my aid immediately. They appeared to be more concerned this time as they began to clear up the mess. "Give her a drink," said the older woman, "and just let her rest..."

The cool water eased the burning in my throat. Once more I began to feel tired. Looking up, I saw the man enter the room carrying a large round object. He placed it on the floor in front of me and picked me up. Placing me in the basket he stroked my head.

"There you are, my little one, have a nap," he said, adjusting the soft fabric lining of the basket. I lapsed into a long sleep, as the events of the day had been too much for me. I was exhausted.

I awoke suddenly: the place was in darkness. I became frightened. The woman must have heard my pathetic whimpering; she entered the room and switched on the light. Picking me up in her arms, she gently caressed me. Dowsing the light, she carried me up the stairs into the bedroom and placed me on the bed. I snuggled up to her as she pulled the bedclothes over her. I could feel the warmth of her body against mine, it reminded me of my mother. I couldn't help thinking of my family as I sank into a deep sleep.

The days passed by quickly, the humans growing increasingly friendly towards me. It was obvious to me that I was here to stay; this was to be my home from now on. I adapted very quickly to their ways, being most careful not to relieve myself in the house. The little girl kept addressing me as Po-Po: I gathered this was to be my name. My mother had always called me pet. I wasn't all that bothered; one name was as good as the rest. The little girl fastened the strange thing around my neck and began pulling on it. I thought this was a new game so I began pulling against it. This did not go down very well with her; she became most upset and began to cry. The man came in wondering what was going on. The little girl whom he addressed as Mary started babbling away at him pointing to the thing tied around my neck. He carefully picked up the other end of it and gently coaxed me towards him. I didn't fight back in case I upset him, I didn't want to see him cry as he had been very kind to me. I followed him up the garden path wagging my tail. He was very pleased with me and gave me lots of praise. I knew now what the thing was for. "Well done Po-Po," he said, handing me over to Mary.

The other dogs in the neighbourhood became very friendly towards me. Mary or one of the other humans would take me out each day for a walk or a game in the park. There was only one dog I didn't take to. He was a big black monster who towered over me. Every time we met he would begin sniffing round me, his big cold nose probing my most delicate parts. However I did meet a nice little dog who looked a lot like myself, except he was black and I was white. We became quite friendly towards each other and I would find myself looking forward to our meetings. The humans seemed to know each other very well and would stay for quite a while in the park, allowing us to play together. He told me his name was Pepe.

"That was my father's name," I said proudly as we lay down on the grass.

"Are the humans good to you?" he asked one day as we walked through the park.

"Yes they are very good to me," I replied. "Are yours?'

He told me he lived in a big house opposite the park and that he always went on holiday with the humans. "What's a holiday?" I asked inquisitively.

He laughed at me. "Don't you know?" he asked. "It's when they pack everything up in little baskets with handles on them and put them in their cars and go and live somewhere else for a short while. Most times it's by the sea."

"What is the sea?" I asked, feeling quite ignorant.

"You will find out shortly," he said, "unless they put you in kennels."

Some weeks later I found the humans behaving quite unnaturally. They began putting their clothes in little box-shaped things and were acting very excited. Mary picked me up: "You are going on holiday with us Po-Po," she said, laughing merrily.

I looked round for a box to put my things in. There was my ball, my rubber bone and lots of other things I had acquired. The man entered the room calling to Mary, "Are you ready?" Picking me up he carried me towards the car. "We must get Po-Po clipped first," he said, passing me to Mary in the back seat. I was a bit confused by it all. There was quite a lot I didn't know about in this world of the humans.

He handed me over to the woman in the shop and left. My heart sank as he disappeared through the door. I struggled to get free, I wanted to go with him but the woman held me firmly. "Come on Po-Po," she was saying, "this won't hurt you."

I trembled as she poured the water over me. It was warm: at least that was something, I thought, as she carefully squirted the liquid over me. Gently she rubbed it into my fur. I could see the water was very dirty as she rinsed it away. I had never had a bath before. It was a new experience to me; I enjoyed it. She rubbed me down with a towel and placed me on a table. The next minute she frightened the life out of me as she switched on the funny-looking machine. The warm air penetrated through to my skin as she gently brushed away. I relaxed, hoping she knew what she was doing. My fur was all fluffy when she had finished with the machine. I felt hot but I certainly felt much better. The next minute she began manoeuvring another strange machine over my body. I watched horrified as my beautiful white fur fell to the floor. I was confused even more when she started shaving my paws. Finally she went to work with the scissors, carefully lifting up my legs one at a time and scissoring underneath and round them. "You look beautiful Po-Po," she said, admiring her work. I felt awful: she had shaved my face and my tail and had cut some fur off the top of my head. I couldn't see myself so I had to take her word for it.

I was glad when I heard the humans come in. I wagged my tail in excitement, feeling very relieved that they had come back for me. I must have looked pretty because they made such a fuss over me. Passing me over to Mary in the back seat of the car the man started it up and away we went. I didn't recognise any of the surroundings as we drove along. Mary whispered in my ear, "We're off on our holidays now Po-Po." I looked out of the window, bewildered: so this was it.

The big moment had arrived; another new encounter lay before me. I felt quite refreshed after the visit to the Poodle Parlour. It hadn't been too bad after all. I must admit they had cut my fur against my wishes but having caught a glimpse of myself in the car mirror I was surprised how smart I looked.

The car sped along the great road at a very fast speed, it was a bit scary but gradually I overcame my fears. It was hot in the car and Mary had opened the window. I stood on her lap and looked out at the green fields as we passed them by. Mary must have been tired because she fell into a deep sleep. Suddenly there was a loud bang and the car began to swerve all over the place. The woman screamed hysterically as the man fought to control the car. Another bang as something bumped into us. The impact lifted the car and it began to turn over. I could feel myself being thrown out of the window as the car spun round. I felt a sickening blow as I hit the road, the pain was excruciating as I rolled over and over. Finally I felt the soft grass beneath me. The car had burst into flames and had come to a halt quite a distance from where I had landed. My head hurt as I tried to get up, then everything went dark.

When I regained consciousness I could hear all sorts of peculiar noises coming from the direction of the car. Once more I tried to get up, the flashing lights and loud sirens was all I heard again. I passed out. The night was cold and my whole body was racked with pain as I lay there slowly coming to my senses. I couldn't help crying out as I tried to lift myself up. It started to rain as slowly I tried to drag myself further into the long grass. There was a discarded container or something lying in the grass, I couldn't quite see what it was but somehow I managed to crawl into it, at least it offered some shelter against the rain which by now was pouring down on me. Feeling very cold and frightened I lapsed into a deep slumber.

Chapter 2

The noise of the heavy vehicles roaring aroused me from my sleep. My whole body felt numb as I tried to ease myself out of the container. At least I was alive, I thought, as with great effort I crawled from my shelter. Peering through the long grass I could see the burnt-out wreck of what had once been the humans' car. My heart sank and I began to vomit. No one could have come out of that alive. My whimpering went on unheard as the vehicles roared past. Realising that I had been lucky to escape the horrible accident I suddenly felt very lonely and afraid. Despite the agonising pain I half-crawled and half-dragged myself away from the scene. The further away from the road I could get the safer I felt. Slowly I made my way through the long grass, not knowing where I was going or what lay ahead.

I could just see the outline of some buildings in the distance as I stumbled clumsily along. Pausing to regain my strength I observed that there were several buildings all nestled closely together. Hungrily and painfully I managed to reach the fence. I could now hear a lot of funny noises coming from the buildings. Once more I summoned all my energy together and stumbled into the nearest one. The effort was too much: I collapsed into a bundle on the floor and passed out. From what seemed miles away I could hear a dog barking. My mind slowly cleared as I opened my eyes. The dog standing over me was one of my own although I couldn't help noticing how scruffy he looked. His constant barking made my head hurt. "Please be quiet," I asked, once more feeling the pain in my body. He suddenly disappeared, much to my relief. Moments later I could hear the sound of footsteps coming towards the building. The dog returned accompanied by a woman human being. Her gentle hands began to stroke my back, I let out a loud yelp as she touched the place where it hurt most. She immediately sensed that I was injured and withdrew her hand.

"Don't worry, she will look after you" the dog said sympathetically. "My name is Dinkie," he said, lying down beside me. "What's yours?"

I looked at him. He couldn't have been much older than myself.

"They call me Po-Po," I replied, "I've been in an accident."

The woman eased her hands under my body and lifted me up gently. I took an immediate liking to her as she carried me towards the house. Dinkie followed. Placing me on the table she bathed me with cool water, allowing a little to run into my mouth. It tasted very refreshing; my throat felt as if it were on fire. With great care she dried me with a towel. "You poor little thing," she said, "I'll have to take you to see the vet."

Once again I felt afraid. Dinkie must have sensed this: jumping up onto the table he said, "She is only going to take you to see the doctor, just to see how bad your injuries are."

The man in the white coat felt me all over. I let out a yelp as he pressed my side. "Seems as if a rib is broken," he said to the woman. I didn't know what he meant of course, but he began to wrap something around my body very tightly, he then reached for a peculiar looking object and stuck it in me. I snarled at him as the thing pierced my skin, it was sharp and I didn't like it very much. The woman handed him some paper from her purse and picked me up. I trembled again as she put me in the car. I hated these contraptions, I never wanted to see another one, let alone ride in one. I felt myself falling into a deep sleep as she closed the door.

Dinkie was at my side when I woke up. "How do you feel now Po-Po?" he asked, looking at me through his kind eyes.

"Oh, I feel stiff all over," I replied. "Where are we, Dinkie?" I asked out of curiosity.

"This is a farm," he said, "I live with the humans, they are very good to me, I do hope they will let you stay."

"What's a farm?" I asked, bewildered.

He laughed at me. "I can see that you are one of those city girls," he said, shaking his head. "A farm is where the humans grow their food and raise other animals," he laughed once more. "When you are feeling better I'll show you around, I'm sure you will like it here."

The woman came in and placed some food in front of me. It smelt delicious. Easing myself up, I began to devour the contents. "You poor little thing, you must have been starving," she said, fumbling with the disc attached to my collar. "Po-Po, that's a lovely name but there's no address on here."

It was quite obvious she didn't know about the accident. If my address had been on it there wouldn't have been anybody there: as far as I knew, all the humans in the car were dead.

The time passed by quickly. Dinkie and I became very fond of each other. We had great fun as he showed me around the farm. I didn't realise such creatures existed as the ones he pointed out to me. The humans were very good to me; they looked upon me as their own and I became attached to them. The man was very nice: he would often pick me up and make such a fuss of me.

"I told you they would look after you Po-Po, didn't I?" said Dinkie as we lay in the barn one night.

"Yes, they are very kind" I said, "they are very much alike my other owners". I felt the tears come into my eyes as I thought of little Mary.

Dinkie must have sensed my sadness he began licking my ear. "I think I must be falling in love with you" he whispered.

As the weeks rolled by I began to think less about that awful event that had brought me to the farm. I began to realise how fond I was of Dinkie. He was very affectionate and we were always together, even on our visits to the Poodle Parlour. I noticed how handsome he looked when he had his fur cut. He would hold his head up high as we walked side by side as if to say: "This is my girlfriend Po-Po." I could feel myself falling for this handsome young dog. He would spend many hours together in the barn; it seemed to be our favourite place.

I suppose really it was inevitable: our relationship grew and our feelings for one another blossomed. Dinkie would often say how much he would like to have a family. It wasn't until I felt the slight movement inside of me that I realised that his wishes were to become a reality. We were in the barn one night as usual, frolicking about in the straw. Dinkie was playing a bit rough so I decided that it was time I told him. I lay down.

"Come here Dinkie," I said mysteriously. I couldn't help laughing at the puzzled look on his face as he bounded over towards me.

"What's the matter?" he asked, lying down at my side.

I looked at him. "Dinkie, you know how you have always said you would like a family," I said to him.

"Yes," he replied.

"Well, you are going to be a father."

He lay there gazing at me. I couldn't help smiling at him. "Do you really mean that?" he asked.

I nodded my head: "Well that's what you wanted, isn't it?"

He leapt into the air as the news sank in, performing one of his favourite somersaults. "Oh, Po-Po," he gasped excitedly, "just wait until the humans find out – they'll be over the moon with delight."

The humans never did find out. We were in the barn one night; it was pretty cold and the wind outside began to get worse. The lantern had always been left alight since the dark nights had come. I suppose the man thought it necessary, as he would often come in at odd times to look around. The wind had really begun to howl; I snuggled up to Dinkie, unaware of the danger we were in. Suddenly the door blew open with such force that the lantern was flung to the floor. The flames leapt all around us; I stood there petrified as they grew higher. We were trapped.

"Po-Po, quickly, come this way!" said Dinkie, tugging at my ear. "There's a hole in the side here; we might be able to get through it if we hurry."

It was a very small hole: I could only just squeeze my small body through it. Dinkie was bigger than me. The barn was now totally engulfed by the flames as Dinkie tried desperately to push his way through. "It's no use Po-Po, I can't make it," he gasped, "save yourself."

I backed away as the heat scorched my coat. "Dinkie!" I cried as the burning timbers collapsed on top of him. I could hear his screams as I raced away from the burning mass. Once again I could see the burning car, my past experience reflecting through my mind as I ran, blindly, into the night.

I wept bitterly as I lay beneath the hedge. I had run myself into the ground in desperation trying to get as far away as possible from the gruesome scene. The night was cold, as I lay there trying to keep warm. I had no idea how far I had travelled, I could only think of poor Dinkie, what a terrible way to die. I began to wish that I had perished with him. The movement inside of me brought me back to my senses. At least I still had a part of him with me. The daylight began to break through the dark clouds. Once more I felt alone and lost. I knew that my babies were due very soon but I didn't know exactly what I was going to do. I had to find more suitable shelter and I had to eat. It began to get warmer as the dark clouds disappeared. Emerging from my temporary shelter, I began to wander aimlessly along the hedgerows.

I could hear the bleating of sheep coming from the field in front of me. I guessed that I must be near another farm so I made my way in that direction. The sheep were grazing peacefully as I made my way towards them. I kept close to the edge of the field not wanting to scare them. Dinkie had often told me how easily frightened they were. I froze in my tracks as the two huge shapes burst through the hedge in front of me. They were the mangiest, meanest couple of dogs I had ever seen, their huge tongues hanging from their mouths as they eyed the sheep in the field. Sensing that something awful was about to happen, I slowly merged into the long grass. The sheep must have sensed it too; they began bleating pitifully and scattered in all directions. The huge savage monsters gave chase. Without realising my reactions I barked as the vicious killers took off after their prey. I watched in horror as the huge beast brought down a young lamb. I couldn't watch as he began to tear away at the lamb's throat. Suddenly there was a terrific bang just behind me. The huge beast leapt into the air; his whole body seemed to break up as he hit the ground, motionless. The other dog had also seized a young lamb and was about to tear it to pieces as the second bang echoed over my head. He fell to the ground, his body covered in blood.

My heart raced as I could hear the footsteps drawing nearer. Realising that my own life was in danger I bolted across the field as fast as my little legs could carry me. There was another loud bang as I reached the hedgerows. I felt the blast as I tumbled through the narrow gap. Pausing to get my breath I ventured to look back through the hedge. The farmer was running towards me with something held under his arm. I could see the smoke coming from it as he fumbled in his pockets. Once again I took to my heels, keeping close to the hedges. I ran as fast as I could until I reached the road. The noise from the traffic frightened me but I couldn't stop: I had to go on.

Chapter 3

Feeling very tired I crawled into a foxhole. Dinkie had told me about foxes and how nasty they were. I peered cautiously into the den. It was deserted. I heaved a sigh of relief as I ventured inside. I remained there for quite a while; I was completely worn out and dozed off. My stomach ached for food as I cautiously crawled out into the bright sunlight. Anxiously I surveyed my surroundings: there was no sign of the farmer or anything else for that matter. Feeling scared once more I began to make my way around the field. As I reached the gateway I could hear a lot of noise coming from somewhere in the next field. Cautiously I crept forward to investigate. There were the sounds of humans and a lot of banging and music. My heart was in my mouth as I edged my way forward; my tummy ached something awful. Lifting myself up on my hind legs, I looked through the hole in the wall surrounding the field. I had never seen anything like it in all my life. The scene in front of me was out of this world.

Sitting down on the grass I began to make plans. I needed food and shelter for the night, that was for sure. Now wherever the humans were there was always food, I knew that, but I was puzzled at the strange sight in front of me. The carts were painted in bright colours and the huge flimsy-looking buildings gently swaying in the breeze were peculiar to me. I had never seen a circus before and my first impressions seemed somewhat apprehensive. My best bet was to lie low until nightfall and then invade the strange camp, hoping to find some food. I nestled myself down in the long grass, noticing the movement inside my tummy becoming increasingly painful. As darkness approached I was suddenly aware that the whole of the camp had been lit up with all coloured lights. It was a pretty sight but I hadn't anticipated this. There were lots of humans milling around the camp and the music was deafening.

Reluctantly I approached the enclosure, my heart beating like a big drum. I could detect a lot of very unfamiliar scents; they were animal scents but none of those I had experienced on the farm. Feeling full of uncertainty I cautiously made my way to the nearest vehicle. It was very large like some I had seen visiting the farm. I kept wishing Dinkie was with me; he would have known what to do. Creeping under the vehicle I viewed the camp more closely. The humans appeared to be enjoying themselves, especially the younger ones. The gaily-coloured lights kept flashing on and off. As I crept by one of the strange-looking buildings I touched it with my paw. It wasn't hard material like the houses I had been in, it was very soft. Of course I was to learn later on that these strange things were called tents. Keeping well into the shadows I made my way around, being careful not to be seen. I could smell food: the hunger in my tummy was really beginning to tell on me. It had been quite a while since I had last eaten and I was getting desperate. With my paw I lifted the flap and peered inside. The floor was strewn with straw; realising that it was now or never, I ventured inside. The huge monster leered down at me as I stood there petrified. It was the biggest animal I had ever seen in my whole life. Its ears were like great wings and its nose reached to the floor.

My immediate reaction was to retreat as quickly as I could. It looked down at me as I stood rooted to the spot. I expected it to attack me but it just stood there looking at me as if I was nothing of importance and gradually my confidence returned and I began to look around, keeping a watchful eye on the huge creature. There was plenty of straw in the tent which I thought would be a good place to spend the night but I was hungry. Once more the smell of food reached my nose. I began to follow the scent. It led me into another large tent where there was a huge cage on wheels. There were some steps leading up to the cage so I began to climb them to see what was in the cage. Peering cautiously through the bars I could see a large piece of meat amongst the straw. My mouth watered as I looked at it. The cage was empty, so with the pangs of hunger tearing at my stomach I eased my small frame through the bars. It was all I could do to drag the meat along the floor. With great determination I gradually manoeuvred it towards the edge of the cage. Using my head I pushed it through the bars, it fell to the floor with a thud. Feeling very pleased with myself I clambered down after it. Again it required all the strength I could muster to drag it back into the tent where the huge monster was. Somehow I had a feeling of trust for this big animal: he made no effort to stop me as I dragged the meat into a quiet corner.

Still keeping a watchful eye on him I attacked the piece of meat, my small but sharp teeth tearing away at it. Feeling much better after the meal I began to gather up the straw around me to make a nice cosy bed. All my strength seemed to leave me as I sank into a deep sleep. I awoke suddenly; the pains in my tummy became very severe. I couldn't help whimpering. I felt terribly ill. A strange-looking human looked down at me as I lay there helpless and in pain. He smiled at me as I bared my teeth at him. The pains became more regular; I was panting heavily. The strange human must have sensed my plight. He stooped down and started talking to me in a soft voice. I couldn't help notice the funny clothes he was wearing, they were far too big for him and his nose was bright red. I had never seen a human with hair that colour either.

It was pure ignorance on my part. I'd never seen a clown before and seeing one for the first time, especially in my condition, I became very nervous. I didn't think he was going to hurt me but one could never tell with humans. The pains continued and I whimpered softly to myself.

The human rose slowly to his feet and left the tent, only to reappear with another human. The woman surveyed me very carefully, she was talking to me very softly but I couldn't understand a word she said. The man left the tent again but the woman sat down beside me, still talking in a strange tongue. A few minutes passed by and then a dog appeared on the scene. She was the same kind as me except for the funny clothes she was wearing. Slowly she approached me, wagging her tail in friendship.

"I'm Mitzi," she said, introducing herself, "and this is Michele my owner, she's very kind; we all belong to the circus."

I looked at her. "My name is Po-Po and I'm very ill," I replied feebly.

Yes, I can see you are having babies," said Mitzi, casting an eye over my swollen body. "Why don't you let Michele help you?"

"Does she know about these things then?" I asked, "because this is the first time I've ever had any and I don't quite know what to do."

Mitzi laughed a little "Of course she does, she's an expert, Michele delivers all our babies, but she is French and her English isn't too good so you may have difficulty understanding her, that is until you get to know her better."

I looked up at the woman; she looked a kind person. "Alright Mitzi, I'll let her help me, tell her I won't bite her."

The dog gave a little yap and rubbed her nose against the human. She seemed to understand what Mitzi was telling her and began gently feeling my tummy. Turning to my new acquaintance she said something and Mitzi ran out of the tent. Within minutes she had returned carrying a little dish in her teeth. I could see that there was some water in it as she lay it at the woman's feet. Gently the woman put the dish closer to me so that I could reach it. I was terribly thirsty and drank quite a lot of water.

Mitzi looked at me. "I think Michele would like to pick you up and take you to our tent," she said, "it's very comfortable in there and you will be much safer."

I could feel the sense of urgency in Mitzi's voice. "That's fine with me," I replied.

Once again the little dog yapped at her owner who seemed to know what she was saying. I felt myself being lifted up by the woman, she was very careful as she carried me into another tent. There were quite a few other dogs in the tent which again made me feel very nervous, but they took no notice as Michele placed me in a basket and put me in a corner well away from the others. I couldn't understand what she was saying except that she kept on referring to me as "My Cheri". For what seemed like hours I lay there; Michele stayed with me. Suddenly I had a funny sensation come over me: I felt as if I was going to burst. Michele began gently pressing my tummy. The sensation passed and I felt the little movements inside. Within minutes my babies were born. There were two of them, as far as I could tell: two little rat-like creatures nibbling at my tummy.

Michele looked after me very well, I thought, considering I was a stranger who had crept into their camp to steal food. She helped me with my two babies, making sure the other dogs kept their distance. The days passed quickly by and soon my strength returned. Michele gave me special food which I needed now that I was feeding two hungry little girls. Every time I looked at them I could see Dinkie, I kept wishing he was with me, he would have been very proud of his daughters. As the time went by I gradually grew accustomed to my new home. The other dogs became very friendly towards me and told me about the circus. Apparently Michele taught them to do tricks which they performed in the big tent to amuse other human beings. I found this a bit strange at first but then one day Michele came in and started showing me how to walk on two legs. I must have had a flair for it because I found it quite easy to do and in fact I enjoyed doing it because it seemed to please her very much. She showed me other tricks that I had seen the other dogs doing. Soon I was a part of the show. My two little girls were also introduced into the act although they played about too much, but they were still very young and full of fun.

The circus travelled around quite a lot going from town to town. It all seemed so pointless to me, I couldn't understand why they didn't stay in one place. Mitzi explained it all to me one day as we were resting in between shows. Apparently the circus needed a fresh supply of human beings for each show. My two little girls enjoyed the circus life very much. I watched them grow up, they were very beautiful girls. Michele called them Cindy and Candy; she was very good with them and they soon became the stars of the show. I felt very pleased as I watched them perform. I'm sure Dinkie would have been proud of them.

One day I was walking around the camp when I came across a new tent. Feeling as if I ought to make friends with whoever lived in it, I walked in. The man glared at me as I entered; I could see that he was holding two fire sticks in his hands. Suddenly he blew onto them and a huge flame shot across the tent towards me. Once again the horrors of my past loomed in front of me. I screamed with fear as I ran from the tent; it was Michele who found me cowering in the corner of our tent, too petrified to move. She couldn't understand what had come over me but from that day on I was never the same. I became a complete nervous wreck. I told Mitzi about my previous experiences and she was very understanding but Michele became very angry with me, I couldn't do my tricks right which infuriated her; eventually she gave up trying to teach me. I was too nervous and couldn't concentrate, in the end I just paraded around the big top to make the number up.

We moved on from town to town. I never could tell where we were; they all looked the same to me. Besides that we never did leave the circus area much anyway, we only caught fleeting glimpses of the countryside when we were on the move. It was on one of these long journeys that Mitzi broke the news to me. We were in the same cage; I noticed how quiet she was and thought she wasn't feeling very well.

"Are you alright?" I asked.

She looked at me with a sad expression on her face, "Yes I'm alright," she replied, "just a bit sad that's all."

It was unusual for Mitzi to act like this so I asked her why she was so unhappy. She shook her head. "It's not fair Po-Po, it's not your fault really but they don't understand do they?"

I looked at her, confused. I didn't really know what she was talking about. "What do you mean Mitzi?" I asked. She turned her head away; I could see that she was crying. "What do you mean it's not my fault?" I was very curious by now and became very persistent.

"They are going to give you away," she cried out. My heart sank; my first thoughts were of my two little girls, I couldn't breathe at the thought of being parted from them.

Mitzi stopped crying and moved closer to me. "I overheard Michele talking to one of the other members of the circus. She said she would have to find a good home for you because you were too nervous to be in the act."

I lay awake all that night wondering what was going to become of me. I cried a lot because I knew I would never see my daughters again, and I was aware of how cruel some humans are. We reached our destination and I waited patiently to see what was going to happen to me. I talked a lot with my two girls, I made up the excuse that I was tired of the circus and would like to live with a human family again.

"Does this mean that you will be leaving us, Mama?" asked Cindy sadly.

I tried to be cheerful about it. "Well yes, it does really, but you mustn't feel too bad about it my angel. I can't be with you forever, you are both big girls now with a good future ahead of you. I myself would like to settle down; I'm getting tired of all the travelling about. I need a rest."

Candy looked at me sorrowfully. "But Mama you can rest and still be with the circus, can't you?"

I shook my head, trying to hide my feelings. "No my angel, the travelling about is making me ill, but I don't want you to start worrying about me: I shall be alright. Now I want you both to promise me that you will make no fuss when I leave, I want you to carry on just as if I were still with you, do you hear?"

They both nodded their heads. I could see that they were both very upset as indeed I was. I left them standing there looking at each other, I hurriedly found a quiet place and had a good cry.

That evening I didn't join in the act; instead I watched from the bandstand. They were really wonderful to watch, my two little girls were now the star attraction in our act; the audience loved them and gave them tremendous applause. I felt happy knowing that they were going to be alright. My only regret was that Dinkie was not there to see them. Mitzi and I had a long talk afterwards. I asked her if she would look after them for me when I was gone.

"I'm going to miss you Po-Po," she said, "we've been such good friends, I do hope we meet up again."

She was very kind but I told her that I doubted very much if we would ever see each other again; my future was very uncertain.

"You never know Po-Po, we may come to wherever you are, the circus travels all over the country. Keep an eye open for the posters, you never know."

I looked at her. "What are posters?" I asked.

She explained that usually the circus advertises by putting up pictures of the circus on walls in the towns where they are going to be at. "You never know Po-Po, some day we may run into each other again, I hope we do."

Chapter 4

The next day Michele came into our tent and picked me up she began talking to me in a very gentle tone I suddenly became aware that something was about to happen as she began to brush and comb my fur. After about five minutes a strange man came into the tent, he looked at me and then began talking to Michele. I couldn't understand what they were saying but I knew this was the moment of my departure from the circus. The man was carrying a small travelling box similar to those Michele put us in when we were travelling; my heart sank as he reached out for me. I didn't like the look of him at all. I was bundled into the box and carried out of the tent, I heard the car door close as I was placed inside. Once again I became very frightened and couldn't help letting out a little whimper. The man immediately bellowed at me to be quiet: I knew then that my destiny was somewhat obscure and that the 'good home' I was supposed to be going to was not to be. I felt sick; we had been travelling for some time now, in what direction I did not know. All that I did know was that I was being taken further and further away from my children and my friends. Eventually I fell asleep,

It was dark when we arrived at our destination. I was awakened by the sound of barking dogs. At first I thought I had been dreaming and that it was all a horrible nightmare. However, it all became a reality as I was transported from the car and taken into a large brick building. The man switched on the light and suddenly the whole place became alive with barking dogs. As I tried to peep through the grill at the front of the box I suddenly felt myself being placed on the ground; the man opened the box and tipped me out. I looked around in amazement. I was in a large pen surrounded by wire mesh. The man placed a bowl of water in front of me then left. I watched as he fastened the door behind him; I know now how the animals in the circus felt being locked up in their cages. Peering through the wire I could see that there were rows and rows of these pens, all fenced off individually and each containing a dog or in some cases two dogs. There were dogs of all shapes and sizes, some of which I had not seen before.

The man bellowed out once again "Quiet!" – that's all he seemed to know – he then put out the lights and locked the outer door. At last the barking subsided, to my relief: I could not have stood it much longer. Having quenched my thirst I began to feel my way around; the straw on the floor was fresh, that was something, but that was about all I could say in favour of my new home. My nose touched the side of the pen as I wandered around in the dark, I could hear the gentle breathing of the dog in the next pen. As I turned to move away I heard a voice call out to me. "Hello there stranger, welcome to paradise."

I paused and looked around. "I beg your pardon," I said, looking through the wire.

"I said welcome to paradise," said the voice.

"Is that where I am then?" I asked inquisitively.

The stranger immediately burst into a fit of laughter, causing all the other dogs to join in. "Did you hear that boys?" he called out. "Is this paradise?"

The whole building was filled with laughter. I felt very embarrassed and moved away to the other side of the pen. Scraping some straw into a pile I settled down, alone with my thoughts. After the laughter had died down I became aware of someone moving around in the next pen; I gave a warning growl to whoever was in there.

"Please don't be angry, I won't hurt you or try and make a fool out of you," came the gentle voice. "My name is Penny, I am a Golden Retriever," she said, introducing herself.

"I am Po-Po and I am a French Poodle, toy one, that is," I replied courteously. "Where exactly are we?"

She moved closer to the side of the pen. "Come a little nearer Po-Po so as I don't have to talk loud – we don't want the others butting in all the time, do we?"

I sensed that Penny was a friendly dog and at that moment I needed a friend because I was feeling very depressed.

"This is a Kennels," said Penny quietly

"Well what do they do here?" I asked curiously.

"Don't you know what kennels are?" she asked, quite amused.

"No I don't, I've spent all my life in the circus," I replied defiantly.

"Oh excuse me, I didn't know," answered Penny apologetically. "Well, this particular kennels is used for breeding," she explained, "the humans find you a mate and expect you to have a litter of babies so they can sell them off to other humans. It doesn't sound very much of a good future, does it Po-Po?"

My heart sank: so this was the good home Michele had found for me. How I hated her. "Have you been here long Penny?" I asked her.

I heard her give a deep sigh. "It seems a long time," she said, "but I think it's only been a couple of months."

We spent quite a long time chatting to each other. Penny told me all about the kennels and the humans that kept them. I must admit I did not look forward to my stay in this place.

The following morning I was awakened by the noise of all the dogs barking. "What's all the fuss about?" I asked Penny who was looking through the wire.

"Oh, the usual morning exercise: the humans take us out into a field and let us run around for a little while, they clean out our pens and prepare the place ready for visitors, they like to create a good impression."

I watched as the dogs were led out in small groups. A young girl came and slipped a lead onto my collar; I was relieved when she put a lead on Penny.

"It looks as if we are going out together," I said.

Penny informed me that all the female dogs were taken out separately to avoid any complications. I agreed that it was a good idea.

"Have you had any children?" I asked her, as we were led into the field.

"No not yet, but I've a feeling that the humans have a mate lined up for me, they brought a young dog to see me a few days ago. I didn't like him though and bared my teeth at him."

We were walked around the field for a while I asked Penny if they ever took the leads off so that we could have a good run around.

"You must be joking," she laughed, "half the dogs here would be off like a rocket. I must admit, though, it would be fun."

We were taken back to our pens after the short exercise. I noticed the wooden peg the young girl used to fasten the door with: it didn't look as if it would be too difficult to open the door should I ever want to.

"Have you ever thought of running away from here, Penny?" I asked casually.

She shook her head. "Run away, where to?" she asked.

"Don't you know where you came from?" I enquired, looking at her mystified.

"Oh yes, I remember alright. I used to live with a human who hardly fed me and never took me out or anything and often he would hit me, especially if I ever had a little accident around the house, you know what I mean?"

I agreed that she was better off in the kennels. "But you haven't really seen much of the outside world, have you?"

She looked at me with curiosity. "What is there to see?" she asked, puzzled by my questioning.

I laughed a little. I couldn't help thinking what a dull life she must have led.

The man who had brought me suddenly appeared at my pen and looked at me. I didn't particularly like the way he was looking at me; I retreated into the back of the pen. He said something to the girl at his side who promptly opened the door and entered, scooped me up in her arms and carried me into a small room inside the building. The man came in as the girl placed me on a table. He began to feel me all over, poking at my head and teeth. Muttering something to the girl, he left the room; she started brushing my fur. I realised I was being groomed for some reason but I wasn't quite sure what. I was bathed and dried and then the girl went to work on me with the clippers. She wasn't very gentle and I let her know by snapping at her, only to receive a sharp smack around my ears. At last she finished and carried me back to my pen.

Penny burst into laughter when she saw me. "Good heavens Po-Po, what on earth have they done to you?" she asked.

"I'm not quite sure yet," I said, looking down at my legs where the fur had been shaved off. I had seen some of the dogs in our act clipped like this and always thought how ridiculous they looked; now I myself looked just as silly. I could understand why Penny laughed.

"Why do you think they have clipped you like that Po-Po?" she asked, trying hard not to laugh.

I shook my head. "I don't know. Besides, my fur isn't long enough for this style anyway."

Penny began asking me all kinds of questions about why I had to have my fur clipped regularly, I told her that if I wasn't clipped my fur would just keep on growing.

"That's funny, mine just drops out now and then, I always thought it was something to do with the weather," she replied, sighing with relief.

At that moment the man walked by with two dogs on a lead.

"Huh, don't speak to those two," said Penny angrily.

"Why, what have they done to you?" I asked.

"Nothing really, but they think themselves special and they get looked after better than any of us," she replied, baring her teeth at them.

"Well there must be a reason for it, maybe they are that man's own pets," I said; "the humans always look after their own dogs better don't they?"

Penny walked away in disgust. "Mine didn't, all I got was a kick now and then."

I lay down in the straw and looked at her. I could see how hurt she was. I began telling her about my first home and how the humans had been so kind to me. I must have rattled on for ages; in fact, I told her my whole life's history.

She listened intently as I went on about the farm. "Goodness me Po-Po, you have had an exciting life, haven't you?"

The dog in the next pen poked his nose through the wire. "Excuse me, but did I hear you say that you had lived on a farm?"

I looked at him. He was a really ugly looking brute; it looked as if his whole face had been pushed in.

"Yes you heard alright, nosey," I said, turning my back on him.

"I used to live on a farm as well," he said. I noticed a sadness in his voice, I looked round and saw the tears running down his face. I felt very ashamed at myself for being so unkind to him; walking up to him, I apologised for being so rude. "Yes, I lived on a big farm for quite a while," he said, sitting down and wiping away the tears with his paw.

"What happened?" I asked. "What brings you here?"

He sighed deeply. "My owner died and there was nobody else to look after me. Nobody wants a boxer because they say we are not very handsome, but we can't help the way we are born, can we?"

I felt sorry for him. "What's your name?" I asked.

"Roger," he replied, "and you are Po-Po. I know I have been listening to you and Penny talking; I'm sorry, I didn't mean to be nosey."

The man walked past again with his two dogs. "You know why they are treated better than us, don't you?"

I shook my head. "No I don't actually, why are they?"

Roger turned his head and watched as they went by. "Because they are show dogs, that's why they get all the attention, look how well-groomed they are." I had noticed what lovely coats they had and how elegantly they walked, "They don't let them mix with us at all," said Roger, stretching his legs. "They think they are superior to us."

I smiled at him, he wasn't a bad sort after all, despite his ugliness. In fact we became very good friends in the days that followed. I began to feel bored in the kennels, there was nothing to do all day except lie about. Eventually I started doing a few somersaults and various other tricks Michele had taught me. That passed away the time a bit and it also amused Roger and Penny.

"You are clever Po-Po, you should still be in the circus," said Penny observing my talents.

I shook my head slowly. "No, those days are over for me now thanks to that dreadful man with the fire sticks, that put an end to my career as a performer. I would like to go and live on a farm again, though. Dinkie and I had a wonderful time together."

Roger nodded his head. "Yes, it is a good life on a farm, I miss the freedom."

The weeks passed by slowly. Occasionally the humans would bring others of their kind and show them around the kennels. Some of the dogs would be taken away and then others would be brought in to replace them, it was all so boring. One day the young girl came to my pen and picked me up and took me into the other room, once again I was bathed and clipped. I had by now grown quite a long mane. The girl began grooming me and snipping away at my fur, finally she tied a piece of ribbon on the top of my head. I was puzzled by all the attention I was getting. Finally the man came in and examined me, he muttered something to the girl and left the room. I expected to be taken back to my pen but instead the girl put me in one of those travelling boxes and carried me outside to the car. I felt very upset, I was being taken away again and I hadn't had chance to say goodbye to Roger and Penny. The man and the girl got into the car and we drove away; I noticed that the two show dogs were in the back of the car and that aroused my suspicion. After a short drive the car stopped: I felt myself being carried into a large building and could hear lots of other dogs barking. I tried to see through the grille in the front of the box: there were lots of humans about and plenty of dogs. The girl placed the box on the ground and lifted me out, putting me onto a table where she began to brush and comb my fur.

I had never been to a dog show before let alone being entered into one. I became very nervous and started to shake. The man came up and inspected me, he nodded his head at the girl and a lead was attached to my collar.

The other two dogs looked at me disapprovingly. "You will never do any good," said one of them, looking me over.

"I suppose this is your first time," said the other one.

"I didn't ask to be showed off," I said abruptly.

"Well you are going to be and you had better be good," said the larger of the two.

"Will I be with you?" I asked nervously.

The dogs burst out laughing at my remark. "What, you with us? Well you are a cheeky beggar, no you won't, they don't have silly little poodles with Alsatians. Don't you know anything about dog shows?"

I told them I had never been in one before and didn't know what to do.

"Well for a start don't get biting the judge who will be looking you over, and stand still while he does it."

The other dog chimed in, "You will be asked to parade up and down so hold your head up high and show off a bit. Mind you, it all depends on whether you've got the right bone structure and a good head.'

I began to shake again, my nerves getting the better of me. I looked up at the two dogs, "I can't help it, my nerves are so bad."

The big dog, whose name was Jason, seemed to understand: "Yes, it can be a bit nerve-wracking at first but don't worry, the master will probably give you a tablet to calm you down a bit."

Sure enough, the man came along and looked at me, he put his hand into his pocket and brought out a bottle containing some pills. He gave one to the girl who popped it into my mouth and made me swallow it. Shortly after the shaking stopped and I felt more relaxed but a little tired. Jason was led off by the man.

I looked up at the other dog. "Aren't you going?" I asked.

He shook his head. "No I don't go in for the beauty lark, I prefer something more challenging," he remarked casually.

"What else is there?" I enquired,

"Oh dear, you are green aren't you, I go in for obedience work. It's far more exciting and much more of a challenge; of course, you need brains for that."

An hour passed by before the man returned with Jason. "Well how did it go?" asked the other Alsatian.

Jason didn't look too happy as the man handed him over to the girl. "Third," he scowled, "some ugly mutt pushed me out of second place just because his coat was better than mine, I should have been first really I was the best dog in the ring. I'm sure that judge doesn't like me".

Rex (the other dog) shook his head: "Well they do have their favourites don't they?"

Jason scowled again. "Next time I'll beat those two pieces of horsemeat, I've got to admit I've seen my coat in better condition than this."

The man came up to us again and took hold of my lead. "It's your turn, kid," said Jason, winking his eye. "Do as I told you, put on a good show and you might just make out."

They both wished me luck as I was led off towards the ring. I was amazed at the number of dogs in the ring. We all looked alike: I couldn't imagine how the humans could tell us apart. The girl stood at the side of the enclosure with Jason and Rex, I guess they couldn't resist the temptation of seeing me make a fool of myself.

We all were led around the ring whilst the judge stood in the middle looking at us. I don't actually know what he was looking for so I just trotted round, holding my head and tail up. After a while he selected about eight of us, the remainder left the ring. I could see Jason standing up; he winked at me encouragingly as we were lined up. The judge walked up and down stroking his chin. I think he was having trouble making his mind up, however he finally indicated to some of the humans who took their dogs and left the ring. I was too frightened to look around but I guessed there were only about three of us left standing there. The judge came up to me and began feeling me all over, he then told the man to run up and down the ring with me. I held my head high and picked up my paws very well. The other handlers did the same with the other two dogs. Finally the judge examined us all again; he nodded to his assistant who started making an announcement to the onlookers. There was a great round of applause as the coloured ribbons were handed out. The master seemed very pleased with me; he picked me up and made a great fuss of me. Jason didn't speak as we joined them but Rex seemed very pleased,

"You did very well for a beginner," he said, looking at the coloured ribbon that had been attached to my collar.

"What does it mean?" I asked, puzzled by it all.

"You came second and that's pretty good," said Rex. "Maybe you have got a good future after all."

We were given a drink and something to eat. Jason eventually came round and began talking to me. "Beginner's luck, that's all," he said, looking down at me. "You haven't really come up against any real competition yet."

I thanked him for his advice, I think he was a bit jealous of me but tried not to show it. After we had eaten and then taken for a little walk, the man took hold of Rex's lead and walked off with him.

"I hope we can go and see him perform" said Jason "he's very good."

The girl held our leads and we followed the man towards the ring. "Good, now you will see a good dog in action," said Jason excitedly.

We watched as the other dogs were put through their paces; it was completely different to what we had to do. Jason explained what was happening as we stood there looking on. The dogs had to do all sorts of things. It was very interesting and I became completely wrapped up in it. It was Rex's turn next, the atmosphere became very intense as Rex and the master entered the ring. I could see by the expression on Jason's face that it was a serious matter.

"How are they doing?" I asked after a little while.

"Shh, be quiet," he whispered as he watched every movement Rex made. I saw the man placing pieces of material down on the floor, it didn't make sense to me at all.

"What are they for?" I asked. Jason looked at me.

"You are dumb ain't you, don't you know anything?"

I explained that it was all new to me. Jason lay down next to me. "You see those pieces of material that the man has put down? Well, one of them has Master's scent on it and Rex has to go and find it."

I thought it quite an easy thing to do actually and told Jason so. He looked angrily at me. "You think everything is easy, don't you, big head? Well it's not, see. The humans try to confuse you by putting other scents down as well but Rex is too good for them: he has a good sense of smell. He ought to be a police dog really, he's an excellent tracker. He could give you a ten-mile start and still track you down."

The crowd applauded as Rex picked up the material and took it back to master. "There you see, he's won," said Jason jubilantly.

Chapter 5

It had seemed an endless day for me. I was feeling very tired as we were taken back to the car.

"Well done Rex," I said as we left the building, "you were very good."

"Oh well, I just happen to be lucky," he said modestly. "Besides, you have done alright yourself today."

The journey home didn't take long and we were soon being led into the kennels again. The girl put me in my pen and I ran up to Penny to say hello.

"So you have joined the aristocrats now," she said rather nastily, "I suppose you will be leaving us peasants and going to live in the house with the others."

I looked at her. I was rather hurt by her remarks. "No Penny I won't, I don't want to leave my friends."

She turned away from me and went and laid down in the far corner of her pen. I walked over to where Roger was lying.

"Hello Roger," I said. He grunted and moved away. I was very hurt my friends had turned against me through no fault of my own.

The following morning the girl came and put my lead on. She had Jason and Rex with her.

"There you are," called out Penny sarcastically, "you don't even exercise with us now. Well goodbye, snob".

Her remarks were very cruel and I was terribly upset. Jason noticed. "Take no notice of those mangy mongrels," he said, laughing out loud, "they are only fit for cat meat anyway."

I looked at him savagely: "Don't you talk about my friends like that or –"

He looked down at me. "Or you will what?"

Rex moved in between us. "Now then you pair, stop this falling out, we are what we are and there's nothing we can do to alter that."

My mind dwelled on what he had said. It was true what he had said. We couldn't help being what we were, I certainly had never asked to become a show dog but I didn't want to lose my friends.

The girl took us back after a while but instead of taking me back to my pen she led me along with Jason and Rex into another building where the man lived. She put me in a large basket with a nice warm blanket on the bottom. She then slipped off my lead and left me alone with Jason and Rex.

"You see we get all the comforts of a proper home," said Jason, wandering freely around the room, "and what's more we are free to roam about instead of being cooped up in those awful pens."

I looked at Rex as he sprawled out in front of the fire, he seemed contented enough and appeared to be quite happy.

"I would still like to be with my friends even if it means being put in a pen," I said. looking at them.

Jason settled down besides Rex. "We're not good enough for her," he replied heaving a deep sigh. "Oh well it takes all sorts, doesn't it?"

I waited for them to drop off to sleep before venturing out of my basket. The door had been left slightly ajar so I quietly slipped through into the yard outside. I could see the big building where all the other dogs were kept. The girl was just coming out; she had her hands full so she could not close the door behind her. I waited until she was out of sight before sneaking across. I held my breath as I entered, hoping that the man wasn't in there. Seeing that there were no other humans around I quickly made for my pen: it was still empty. Penny looked up as I approached. She immediately turned her head away and retreated to the far corner.

"Penny, please speak to me," I begged, trying to keep my voice down, "I didn't ask for all this attention. I wish they would leave me alone and let me come back in here."

Penny didn't say anything, she just lay there ignoring me. I looked into Roger's pen: he was asleep.

"Roger wake up please, let me talk to you."

He opened his eyes and stared at me. "Why don't you buzz off to where you belong? You are not one of us anymore." His eyes closed again.

I was deeply hurt by his remark. "Roger please don't blame me, I don't want to be like those others I want to be here with you and Penny. I miss you both very much, you are my real friends."

The tears began to trickle down my face, I was so upset. Penny stood up and stretched her legs; she looked at me through the wire. "Oh don't start that," she said coming closer, "we know it's not your fault really – it's those stupid humans they can be very cruel at times."

Roger opened his eyes again and looked at me. "We know, Po-Po, it's not your fault, but they won't let you come back here now, you are a show dog and you will be treated better, why don't you make the best of it?"

Penny looked at Roger. "Okay Po-Po, we will still be friends but I doubt if we will ever be able to mix now."

I thanked her for being so understanding. I felt very relieved. "I'll come and see you whenever I can," I said.

Roger winked his eye at me. "Take care, Po-Po. If the humans find you in here they will punish you. I think you had better go now." I leapt for joy as I made my way back to the house.

"Where have you been?" asked Jason suspiciously as I crept back into my basket.

"Only outside for a little walk," I replied returning his stare. "You had better behave yourself, you know, or the master will smack you."

I settled down for the rest of the evening, feeling a little happier in myself. It was nice to know I hadn't lost my friends. A few days later I was busy re-arranging the blanket in my basket when I heard several humans laughing outside the house; well naturally I was curious so I crept to the door and peeped out. There were four of them including Master standing there talking and laughing, but my eyes rested on the white dog they had with them. He was a poodle like me. He also had his fur clipped like me which I thought made him look a bit stupid, I mean it's alright for us girls to have fancy clips but not for a boy. The master came into the house and slipped on my lead, taking me outside to where the humans were. The women made a great fuss of me but the man who was with them seemed more interested in feeling me all over and carefully examining me.

The dog suddenly became interested in me. "Hi ya there kiddo, how's tricks?" he said in a cocky tone.

"My tricks are alright thank you, not that it is any concern of yours," I replied, moving away.

The master gave a jerk on the lead, bringing me face to face with the dog again, "So you are the lucky girl then," he laughed, sniffing around me.

I moved away again. "What do you mean, lucky girl?" I asked curiously.

"Gee whizz kiddo you are green, don't you know why I've been brought to see you?" he smirked.

I shook my head. "No I don't know, and will you please keep your nose to yourself?"

He was a cheeky dog and very persistent so I snapped at him, this brought a clip around the ears from the master. "It's no use kiddo, it has to be. You should consider yourself lucky really. I am very famous and have sired many good puppies."

The thought sickened me. No way was I going to subject myself to this bigheaded bag of bones. Once again I snapped at him, again being rewarded by a clip round the ears. The master had me back into the house and shouted at me, lashing me with the lead. I crawled into my basket feeling very sore. I knew that I had to get away from the kennels if I was to save my dignity.

I lay in my basket all day wrapped up with my thoughts. I was beginning to feel as depressed as ever. Rex came in and lay down in front of me.

"What's the matter?" he said, looking at me, "you don't seem very happy."

I knew I was taking a risk in letting him into my confidence but at that moment I was so unhappy I needed someone to talk to.

"I would like to get away from here Rex," I said, watching his reaction.

He stared at me. "Don't try it Po-Po, please, don't try it," he said, looking very serious.

"Why not?" I asked.

He turned his head away from me. "Because the master would send me after you, that's why, and I would have to come and find you and you know very well I could."

My heart sank. I didn't realise how stupid I had been in letting Rex into my secret. I couldn't have told anyone more dedicated to his work than Rex. I pretended to dismiss the idea entirely and told him about the dog who had been brought to see me.

"We don't have much choice in such matters really, the humans seem to arrange everything for us," said Rex understandingly, "but I would try and make the best out of it, Po-Po. The humans will treat you well."

That evening I managed to sneak out of the house again. There was a full moon shining as I made my way across the yard to the kennels. I tried to open the door with my paw but it would not open; I looked up and saw that the catch was on. I was about to return to the house when I noticed a metal container lying on its side, it looked very much like the ones we used to roll about in the circus. I nudged it and to my delight it began to roll, I became very excited as I rolled it towards the door. I realised that my experience with the circus had not been in vain. The container came to rest. All I had to do now was to stand it on its end, this was the difficult part. I stood up and placed my front paws on the end of the container and pulled. Slowly it began to tilt: I backed away, pulling at the same time with my paws. My heart beat faster as it came to rest in an upright position. I could not help the noise it made as it rattled on the concrete floor; this caused one of the dogs inside to start barking. Fearing that someone in the house may have heard the noise, I took cover and waited. No one came out so I assumed that they had not heard anything. I waited until the dog stopped barking before I dared to continue.

Jumping up onto the container I reached for the catch on the door; to my disappointment I wasn't tall enough to reach it. I stood there with my heart in my mouth. I wasn't going to give up now, so I began to look round for something to reach the catch with. Once again my circus training proved to be of great assistance: I picked up a stick in my mouth and jumped up onto the container; carefully I reached for the catch. I was relieved to hear it click as I pushed upwards. The door was now open. I jumped down and gently pushed the container away from the door. Opening the door a little more I peered inside: it was very dark in there. Cautiously I crept inside. The second door was also closed. I looked up at the handle: it was different to the one on the outside door. It wasn't so high up as the other one so I figured that with the help of the container I would be able to reach it. Slowly I tipped it over, it made a terrible noise as it clattered on the hard floor. Once again the dog began to bark inside. I kept hoping that he would shut up. Finally he gave up, much to my relief: I knew that if the humans had come to see what all the commotion was about I would really be in for it. Once again I began to roll the container inside the building. The straw on the floor deadened the sound as I struggled to upright it.

A sigh of relief escaped my lips as my paw pressed down on the handle: the door opened quietly. Jumping down, I pulled at the door with my paw, opening it just wide enough for me to enter. Penny was asleep as I looked at her through the wire.

"Psst, Penny," I called out, trying not to rouse the other dogs. She stirred a little but apparently she had not heard me. "Penny, wake up," I whispered.

"Who's that?" she asked sleepily.

"It's me, Po-Po, I must talk to you."

She ambled over to the door of the pen. "What on earth are you doing here at this time of night?" she asked, giving a yawn.

I told her what had happened. She listened as I revealed my plan to escape.

"You must be mad," she said, "How on earth can you escape from this place and where would you go?"

I explained how I had opened the doors and how easy it would be for me to open the door of her pen.

"Now just hold on a moment Po-Po, who said anything about me coming with you?"

I looked at her. "Do you really want to spend the rest of your life here?" I asked.

She thought for a moment. "But where would we go?"

I shook my head. "I don't know yet Penny, but anywhere would be better than staying here."

A movement in the next pen made me jump. "It's only Roger," whispered Penny, "the humans have put him in your old pen."

Roger poked his nose through the wire. "What's all this I've been listening to, are you really planning to escape, Po-Po?"

I assured him that he had heard right.

"Where will you go?" he asked. I noticed a hint of enthusiasm in his voice.

"Are you interested?" I asked.

"You bet I am, I'm absolutely fed up with this life, but how on earth can we escape?"

I told him that I had it all planned out. "We can find a nice farm where the humans would look after us," I said.

"Yes that would be great, I would like to live on a farm again I miss the freedom."

I think Roger was excited as I was at the thought of being free again. The more I thought about it, the more determined I became; in fact, I was obsessed with the idea. There was only one problem, and that was Rex.

"I must go now but I'll be seeing you again soon."

Penny pushed her nose through the wire. "Do be careful, Po-Po. Don't get into trouble."

I made my way back to the house, making sure that I had not left anything lying around that would arouse suspicion. I managed to close the doors behind me and rolled the container out of sight.

Jason looked at me suspiciously as I entered the house. "Been for walkies again?" he said in a sarcastic tone.

I ignored his remark and curled up in my basket. The following day we were lying on the grass outside the house, it was a lovely sunny day. Jason and Rex stretched themselves out, idling away the time. Jason casually remarked how he was looking forward to the next show.

"It's important for us show dogs to look after ourselves," he said, licking his paws.

"I'm glad I don't have to worry about my appearance," joked Rex. "My brains are more important."

I listened to them as they both aired their views. I couldn't help thinking how conceited they both were.

"Is there anything you can't do Rex?" I asked as if bored by it all.

Jason laughed out loud. "Yes, there is, he can't use that precious nose of his when it's raining."

Rex growled at him, "No that's true, but you don't look too special either when you are soaking wet."

My eyes lit up as they went on arguing: at last I had discovered Rex's weakness. My mind suddenly became active again as the valuable piece of information sunk into my head.

The days passed by. I knew that very soon the humans would be bringing that horrible dog to me. Somehow I had to shake off Jason's suspicions: my evening walkies, as he referred to them, were becoming too regular.

"What's that tiny wooden hut outside the door for?" I asked casually, having noticed it on several occasions.

"That's a kennel," said Rex. "The master used to keep a guard dog there at one time but it died and nobody has used it since. Besides, who wants a guard dog with us around?"

Jason looked at me. "What do you want to know that for?" he enquired suspiciously.

"Well it's lovely and cool out there. I sometimes go in there out of the sun, in fact I like it very much I wonder if the master would mind if I used it more often. Sometimes it gets too warm for me in the house at night."

Jason didn't say anything but I knew he was suspicious. I decided to let the humans see me in the kennel as often as I could, hoping they would eventually get used to the idea. The man didn't seem to mind; in fact, one day he cleaned it out and put another blanket inside. I thought that was very decent of him and showed my appreciation by licking his hand.

The girl seemed very amused by it. "So you have found yourself a new home Po-Po," she said, looking inside, "but you won't find it very warm when the cold weather comes."

Little did she know my occupation of the kennel wasn't to be for long.

I kept Penny and Roger informed of my activities. "You are clever Po-Po," said Penny, "don't the humans suspect anything?"

I shook my head: "No my dear, they are a bit thick, you know".

Roger kept asking me when the great moment was to be. "You will have to be patient Roger," I told him, "and be ready to move out at a moment's notice."

They both agreed that everything would be left to me.

"But why must we go when it's raining?" asked Penny, adding that she didn't like getting wet.

I told her the reason why and pointed out how important it was.

"Okay by me, I don't mind a drop of rain," whispered Roger.

"Right then, everything depends on the weather," I said. "Oh by the way, make sure you eat up all your meals – we may have to go without for a day or two until we get away. You know everything depends on how fast we can travel once we get away from here."

They both promised to do exactly as I had instructed them. I could sense how excited they were, as indeed I was myself.

Two more days passed by. I looked up at the cloudless sky hoping to see those dark black clouds that usually preceded the rain: there was none to be seen. I felt very much on edge knowing full well that any day now, the humans would be bringing that bag of bones to see me. That evening, as I was eating my meal, a sudden bang startled me.

"What was that?" I asked Rex, who was just finishing his food.

"Sounds like lighting," he said, raising his head and listening. "Don't be frightened, it doesn't hurt you but if I were you I would stay in tonight. I think we are in for a storm."

I looked at Jason who had finished his meal and was curled up on the rug. He was fast asleep.

"I'll just go out for a while before it starts. I don't want to get my coat wet," I said, casually walking towards the door.

I noticed that the man's car was not where he usually kept it. I felt very excited as I walked around the yard; I peered into the big shed where he sometimes put it. To my relief it was not there. I waited patiently for it to start raining. It began to get dark suddenly as the big clouds rolled over. Another loud bang thundered down from the sky, causing me to run across the yard to my little hut.

I waited patiently as the rain began to fall. It was all I could do to stop myself from barking at the lightning as it lit up the sky. The girl came running across the yard from the kennels; she looked into my little hut.

"Come on Po-Po, let's take you inside," she said, stooping down and reaching for me. I growled at her. "Alright then, stay out here if you want to," she shouted, and disappeared into the house.

I waited a moment to see if she was going to come out again. My poor heart felt like a big drum banging away inside of me as the minutes went by. It was now or never, I thought, as I emerged into the pouring rain. Dashing across the yard, I collected my equipment which I had kept carefully concealed; I began to tremble with excitement as I put into action my carefully arranged plan. The tension was building up in me as I rolled the container through the second door. I could feel a hundred eyes watching me as I eased myself into the large building, rolling the container in front of me. I manoeuvred it into position in front of Roger's pen.

Carefully I turned it on its end and climbed on top; I felt blindly for the peg which secured the door.

"Okay Roger," I whispered as the peg fell to the floor, "wait a moment until I can let Penny out."

I repeated the process, trying very carefully not to make any noise. Penny stood there watching as I felt for the peg. To my relief it fell silently to the floor.

"Right Penny, follow me, but be very quiet."

Chapter 6

I could hear Roger breathing very heavily as we crept quietly through the outer door. Penny kept very close to me as we made our way across the yard.

"Which way do we go?" she asked nervously.

I told them to stay very close to me as we travelled down the long drive. "I think we had better cross over the field where they exercise us," I panted excitedly.

The sudden flash of lightning lit up the whole sky, causing Penny to cry out.

"Shh, you must be quiet – it won't hurt you."

We ran across the field and crawled through the hedge into the next one.

"Right, now listen to me very carefully both of you, this lightning doesn't hurt you although it sounds very frightening. Now, we must keep close to the hedgerows and run as fast as we can but stick together or else we will get separated."

I could tell that they were frightened. Little did they realise that I was also scared. The rain came down heavily and soon we were all very wet.

"Can't we shelter for a while?" gasped Penny frantically as we raced along the edge of the field.

I looked at her. She was rather plump and had a thick coat on her that seemed to weigh her down. Every now and then the lightening would flash across the sky illuminating all around. I was very wet myself – the long mane made it very difficult for me – so I knew how Penny must have felt.

"We will rest for a short while," I said, crawling under the thick hedge, "but we must get as far away as possible while it is still raining, that's very important. We don't want Rex on our trail, do we?" They both agreed that it was the last thing they wanted. "Right then, as soon as we have got our breath back we must carry on. The further away we are the better our chances."

Penny was panting very heavily, poor thing. She had more weight to carry than Roger and myself.

"How far do you think we have travelled, Po-Po?" asked Roger, wiping the rain from his eyes.

"I'm not sure but we must go on." I glanced at Penny. I could tell she was exhausted. "It's lack of exercise Penny, you can see what being kept up does for you." She didn't hear me; she was fast asleep.

"Poor Penny," whispered Roger, "she's really out of condition, isn't she?"

I crept from under the hedge and listened. Apart from the usual night-time noises all was quiet. "We'll let her rest for a little while, Roger. I don't think we are being followed yet."

I must have been more tired than I thought for I also fell into a deep sleep. A sudden noise near to us quickly aroused me.

"It's alright Po-Po, it's only a rabbit. I have been keeping watch. Shall I go after it? We may need some food later on." Roger stood up and peered through the hedge.

"No Roger, we mustn't think of food yet. We must carry on." I gently nudged Penny. "Come on love, we must go now."

She yawned and stretched herself. "Thank you Po-Po, I feel much better now. Is it still raining?"

I looked up at the sky. It was beginning to get light. It was still raining but not quite so heavily.

"Yes, but not so much," I said, looking at her. "How do you feel now, Penny? Are you fit enough to go on?"

She gave a little shiver. I too began to feel the cold and I knew Roger must have because his coat was very smooth.

"Which way do we go from here?" she asked, adding that a little run would soon warm us all up.

I peered through the hedge. 'We must keep on going straight across those fields. I don't know for sure where we will end up, I think we will have to trust our luck."

Roger led the way. I felt sure that he must be tired; after all, he had kept a look out while Penny and I had slept. We travelled at a steady pace so as not to exhaust ourselves. The rain had stopped now and the sun had begun to peep through the clouds which helped dry us out. I suggested that we avoid the towns and keep to the countryside· Roger said what a great feeling it was to be free again. I had to agree with him: it was wonderful.

We had been travelling for quite some time now. I felt confident that our escape had been a successful one and informed the others of my feelings.

"We can slow down a bit now I think," I said, lying down in the tall grass. "How are you both?"

Roger stood over me beaming with delight. "I feel fine; how about you, Po-Po?"

I managed to smile at him. I could see he was enjoying all this. "How are you, Penny?" I asked, rolling over on my back and kicking my legs in the air.

"Oh Po-Po, isn't it great to be free? I do hope we can find a nice farm where the humans will take us all in."

The thought had crossed my mind also, but I knew in my heart that the humans wouldn't want all three of us. But I kept my feelings to myself; I could not spoil the happy expressions I could see on their faces.

"I bet they are going bananas at the kennels by now," laughed Roger.

"Well even if we get caught we can always remember our spell of freedom" said Penny with a sigh.

We continued our journey, being careful to avoid any human dwellings. I knew that as the day wore on we would have to find some food and also shelter for the night.

"I'll try and catch a rabbit," said Roger, scanning the hedgerows. "I bet there's plenty about here."

I warned him to be careful and not to take any chances. Penny and I watched as he disappeared through the hedge. "I do hope he catches one," said Penny hopefully.

We waited patiently for Roger to return. The sun was now high in the sky. I knew that by now the humans would have missed us and would be searching the countryside for us. After a while Roger reappeared with a young rabbit in his mouth. He beamed with delight as he dropped it in front of us.

"I'm sorry but it is only a small one," he said apologetically. "The bigger ones were too fast for me."

Penny licked her lips as we ate our fill. "Hmm, that was very nice Roger you did very well," she said, winking her eye at him. "I can see we won't starve as long as you are with us. I could do with a drink now," she added, looking at me.

I asked Roger if he had seen any streams or pools.

He shook his head. "No, but there are some woods just across the fields. I'm sure we may find something there, Po-Po."

We decided to investigate.

Staying close to the edge of the field, we made our way into the woods. Apart from the usual wildlife there was no sign of any humans, which was very encouraging. I suggested that we split up and search the area. Roger agreed that it was a good idea.

After a short while I heard Penny give a bark. I found her standing beside a small stream. "Well done Penny," I said, lapping up the cool water.

Roger appeared shortly and quenched his thirst. "What now, Po-Po?" he asked, shaking his head.

I sat down and thought for a while. It was still early in the day. There was still plenty of time for us to travel, so I suggested that we carried on through the woods, hoping that we could find somewhere to hide for the night.

"This is fun isn't it, Po-Po?" called Roger, leading the way through the trees. I could see that he was really enjoying himself. Penny also appeared to be in good spirits. I was excited myself: it was the first time in a long while that I had enjoyed so much freedom.

"How far do you think we have come?" asked Penny, running alongside of me. I told her that I wasn't sure but guessing by the amount of time we had been on the move I reckoned we had covered quite a few miles.

We eventually came to the edge of the woods. Roger looked at me inquisitively. "What now?" he asked.

I looked out across the open fields. "I think we had better rest for a while; it would be better to wait until it gets dark before we go any further," I suggested.

Penny agreed that a nice rest would be welcome. "I do feel a bit puffed out," she said, lying down.

Roger and I talked quietly as Penny fell into a deep sleep. I told Roger to have a nap as well, adding that I would stay on guard. He soon joined Penny. I listened to them breathing heavily. I must admit Roger had been marvellous: he had been on the go since we had escaped. I don't know where he got all his energy from. I let them sleep for a long time. I had to smile as Roger whimpered excitedly in his sleep; he must have been having a lovely dream.

Penny woke up first and stretched her legs. "Oh dear, Po-Po, I must have been asleep for hours; it's dark, isn't it?"

I gazed up at the stars: I thought of the many nights Dinkie and I had spent together wondering where they all came from.

Roger gave a big yawn as he opened his eyes. "Is it time for us to move on?" he asked, shaking himself.

I suggested that it would be as well to move on. "The further away we get the better," I said, looking at them both. Once again we began to travel. We set ourselves a steady pace so as not to tire ourselves out.

We were very careful when we came to any roads. We looked and we listened before crossing them. I knew the humans drove their cars at night and they would suddenly appear out of nowhere.

Roger called us to a halt. "There are some buildings over there and there are some lights on. Shall we go around them, Po-Po?"

I looked through the hedge carefully. It was getting a little chilly. "It looks like a farm," I whispered.

"I will go and have a look round," said Roger, slipping away into the darkness.

"I do hope he will be alright," sighed Penny.

We waited for a while. Roger suddenly appeared: "It is a farm and there's a nice big barn filled with straw, what do you think, Po-Po?"

I gazed at the buildings. It would be nice if we could spend the night in a nice warm barn.

"Did you see any humans or dogs?" I asked Roger.

He shook his head. "No, it was all very quiet."

We crept forward, letting Roger lead the way. The barn looked very inviting as we slipped quietly through the partly opened door. My first thought was to look for another door at the back of the barn; once again I couldn't help thinking of how Dinkie and I had been trapped. The door was closed but on further investigation I found a window that was open; there was also a bale of straw underneath it so if we did have to make a quick getaway the opportunity was there.

I re-joined Penny and Roger. "This will do fine," I said, curling up in the straw.

The noise of the cockerel crowing roused me from my dreams: it was just breaking light.

"Psst, Roger, Penny."

They blinked their eyes. "Oh what a lovely dream I had," said Penny, stretching her legs.

Roger stood up and looked around. "I'm going to have a quick look round, stay here a minute."

He disappeared before I could say anything, returning almost immediately with an egg in his mouth. "Here, this is for you Po-Po." He disappeared again.

"Here you are Penny." He dropped the egg in front of her.

"What about you?" I asked.

He broke into a broad grin, "I've just had two," he said sheepishly.

We broke the shells and devoured the contents. "That was lovely, Roger," I said, giving him a peck on the nose. He turned away to hide his embarrassment. "We will have to go now," I said, looking at them both. "If we get caught we will be in trouble. Roger, take a look see if anyone is about."

He came bounding back. "The door of the house is open, so I expect the humans are around somewhere. What shall we do?"

I led them to the open window: "This way, follow me."

I leapt upon the bale of straw and jumped through the window. Roger followed immediately. Penny had difficulty but eventually managed it. We kept out of sight of the house and made for the fields, keeping close to the hedges.

The days were long and the nights were cold. Sometimes we were fortunate enough to find shelter in a barn or some sort of building, but some nights we were forced to sleep out in the open. The weather was variable. I looked at my two companions as we huddled together beneath the hedge sheltering from the rain. I could feel the pangs of hunger gnawing at my insides; it had been two days since we had last eaten.

Roger looked at me sadly. "I'm sorry Po-Po, but those rabbits are very fast. I just couldn't catch one this time."

I assured him that it wasn't his fault. He had done his best, but I knew now that we couldn't carry on this way much longer. It was time to find ourselves a proper home with the humans. Poor Penny looked very weary; I could tell she was not feeling very well, although she tried hard not to show it. We waited for it to stop raining: as we sat there shivering, I revealed my plans to them.

"How will we know if the humans want us or not?" asked Penny, hardly able to atop her teeth from chattering.

"It's all going to be a matter of luck," I said hopefully.

I took Roger to one side and pointed out to him that we would have to consider Penny first. He agreed without hesitation. That was the sort of dog he was: very considerate and very understanding.

The sun came out again, drying out our coats and bringing the very much welcome warmth. We sat at the side of the field, gazing down at the farm. It looked quite big; there were lots of buildings and plenty of livestock in the surrounding fields.

"How do we go about it?" asked Penny wearily.

"You will have to approach them very carefully," I said, looking at her. "Don't go near the animals and don't frighten the humans by being aggressive. You will have to rely on your senses: if you feel they are friendly, approach them carefully and wag your tail. If they like you they will try to stroke you. If they do that roll over on your back and let them tickle your tummy, the humans like doing that."

Roger and I watched as she slowly approached the farm, she wasn't very confident in herself and was very reluctant to go. The farm's dog came rushing from one of the buildings, making straight for Penny. Roger jumped up ready to go after her.

"Wait a moment, Roger," I begged him, "let's wait and see what the humans do."

We watched as the farmer appeared from the house. He called the dog, who immediately lay down on the spot. Our hearts were in our mouths as the man approached Penny. He appeared to be quite friendly at first, but suddenly he picked up a stone and hurled it at her. We heard her yelp out as the stone caught her in the stomach. The dog immediately got up and went for her. Roger bounded up and was gone in a flash to her rescue.

I watched helplessly as he quickly covered the ground. In no time at all he was at the dog's throat. Penny limped away whilst they were fighting; I called out to her as she stumbled towards me. The man ran back into the house; I called out to Roger, but I don't think he could have heard me. The man reappeared carrying one of those dreadful bang-sticks. I called out to Roger but he was tearing away at the dog; my heart beat faster as I saw the man running towards them. He gave a loud whistle: his dog tried to shake off Roger, but he could not. Finally he fell to the floor and lay there, very still. Roger looked up at the man as he approached him. I could sense what Roger had in mind, so I called out as loud as I could for him to run. He turned and started to run towards us. The man lifted his arm up and there was a terrific bang. I watched horrified as Roger was lifted up into the air by the impact. He hit the ground hard; he tried to struggle to his feet. There was a second bang as the man walked up to him. I turned my head away as the blood spurted from his body. He gave a loud cry and fell dead.

Penny was crying with pain when she reached me. I was being sick, it was horrible to watch. "Oh Po-Po, what happened?"

I was too upset to answer her. I began to run away. I could hear Penny crying as she followed me. I ran blindly, gripped with fear and horror. I finally collapsed, exhausted; I managed to crawl into the long grass to hide. Penny eventually found me and together we cried, oh how we cried. We spent that night hidden away in the grass. Fortunately it did not rain. We never spoke to each other all night; we only cried to ourselves. I vowed from that moment on that I would kill any human that ever tried to touch me. I awoke to the sound of the birds whistling overhead, the night had been cold and I had snuggled up to Penny to keep warm. I noticed the nasty cut in her side where the man had caught her: it must have been a very sharp piece of stone that he had hit her with. Her coat was soaked with blood and some of it had run into my fur, I looked at the wound in her side; the blood was still seeping from it.

She raised her head slowly and looked at me. "Was it all a bad dream, Po-Po?"

I shook my head. "No Penny, it wasn't a dream, it was real." I felt the tears coming again.

"Where's Roger?" Penny asked. I didn't know what to say to her: obviously she wasn't aware of all that had happened.

I tried to explain what had happened. Penny had been too busy trying to escape from the man. She hadn't seen Roger fighting off the dog or the horrible aftermath. She cried bitterly when I had finished telling her. Her whole body shook with emotion which caused the wound in her side to bleed more. I tried to keep her as calm as possible, knowing that something had to be done to stop her from bleeding to death.

"Can you stand up at all Penny?" I watched as she staggered to her feet.

"I feel very week Po-Po," she said.

I told her to lie down again and to keep very still. I had to find something to cover up the wound in her side with. I crept out of our hiding place and began to look around.

I searched and searched the hedges and all around the field but couldn't find anything. Finally I gave up and returned to where Penny lay. "I can't find anything at all," I said, lying down beside her. For the first time in my life I felt absolutely helpless: my friend was bleeding to death and there was nothing I could do.

I lay my head down in the grass. Suddenly an idea came into my mind. I began to chew the grass, much to Penny's amazement. I chewed quite a bit before spitting it out. Penny looked on as I chewed some more. Gradually I had accumulated quite a pile which I began to place on the wound in her side. She asked me what I was doing; I told her that I was trying to stop the bleeding. She lay there as I applied the dressing; I felt her wince as I applied another layer.

"Be patient Penny, I'm not sure if this will work but I must do something."

I kept on chewing more grass and placing it over the wound; eventually I had applied quite a thick layer of it. "We must now wait and see."

Penny closed her eyes and went to sleep, much to my relief. I was feeling very hungry. I watched the birds circling overhead which gave me an idea. When I lived on the farm with Dinkie, the cats often caught birds and ate them. I crawled on my belly towards the hedge. Suddenly a rabbit darted out in front of me, taking me by surprise. I watched as it disappeared through the hedge. I chased after it but it disappeared down a hole. I perched myself above the entrance and waited patiently for it to reappear. After what seemed an eternity I heard a movement: I stood poised ready to spring.

The young rabbit poked its head out and I sprang, sinking my teeth into its neck. There followed such a scuffle that it felt as if I was fighting a lion. After a while it stopped fighting. I hung on, not knowing whether it was dead or not. It took all my strength to haul it to where Penny lay but I finally made it. Penny was still asleep so I began to tear away at the rabbit. When she woke up she found a nice piece of meat waiting for her. I watched as she ate it ravenously. The wound in her side had stopped bleeding: I told her not to move around too much in case it started again. The chewed up grass had stuck to the wound and dried up; I was very pleased with my work. We spent another night huddled up close together in the long grass but I knew that we could not stay there forever. Somehow we had to find another hideout, somewhere warm. I woke up to find it was still very dark. Penny was sound asleep; I left her lying there as I made my way through the long grass. I couldn't help feeling guilty: Roger was dead and Penny badly injured; it was all my fault, there was no one else to blame. I could smell the cows in the field so I moved very slowly. I knew that somewhere in the field I would find a water trough and I was certainly very thirsty. To my relief the trough stood by the gate; I stood up on my hind legs and drank some of the cool water.

I knew that Penny was in a bad state and couldn't survive if we didn't find some warm shelter. My instinct told me that somewhere near there would be another farm. Usually the cows were kept in a field close by so as they could be fetched in for milking. I wandered round, looking for the buildings. I climbed through the gate which led into a narrow lane. It was starting to get light as I continued my search. Cautiously I approached the farm; it wasn't a very big one and the buildings looked old. By the time I had plucked up enough courage to find out if it was a safe place the cockerels were already crowing. I knew that soon the humans would be up and about. I avoided the cow shed, knowing well that the cows would be shortly be rounded up and brought in. My eyes focused on the big barn where all the straw was stacked: it wasn't all closed in like other barns I had seen, it was open at the front. I ran across the yard and slipped quietly inside. The straw smelt lovely and inviting: a perfect place to hide. I hurriedly retraced my steps to where I had left Penny. She was still sleeping.

I prodded her gently. "Penny, try and get up. I have found somewhere nice and warm for us."

She slowly opened her eyes. "I do feel weak Po-Po, but I will try."

I did all I could to help her to her feet. "Good girl Penny, now follow me."

She winced as she tried to walk; the pain must have been awful. We managed to cross the field, although Penny almost passed out a couple of times.

"It's not much further," I said, trying to encourage her.

She heaved a deep sigh of relief as we crept into the barn. I led her right inside and found a nice warm spot for her,

"There you are love, I'm sure we will be alright here," I said, hoping that I had not made another terrible mistake.

Chapter 7

We hid ourselves deep amongst the straw, waiting to see what would happen. I had been so preoccupied that I did not notice that the wound in Penny's side had opened up again, but as it grew lighter I saw the pool of blood. The walk had tired her out and she was sleeping again. Poor Penny, she looked so thin. I knew that something had to be done for her. I had done all that was possible, but it was not enough. I watched as a man brought the cows in through the gate: all kinds of thoughts raced through my mind as I lay there beside Penny. I nudged her gently. She opened her eyes a little; I could see that she was very weak.

"What is it, Po-Po?" she asked feebly.

I told her that I was going to try and get help; I knew that it was a great risk but something had to be done. I told her that I was going to get the humans to come and have a look at her.

She looked very nervous. "Will they be kind to us?"

I told her that I would hide so they would only find her. "I'm sure they will look after you, Penny, there's nothing else I can do for you."

I waited until I saw the man come out of the cow shed; I let out a loud yelp before burying myself in the straw. The man looked up as he crossed the yard. I let out another yelp. That did the trick: he looked suspiciously towards the barn, then came to investigate.

I watched as he searched the barn; my heart was in my mouth as he drew near. A look of surprise crossed his face as he looked down at Penny. I held my breath as he bent down over her. it was difficult to tell with the humans – some were very kind, but there were some like the one that had killed our dear friend Roger. He spoke quietly to Penny. As he began to stroke her I sensed he was a kind person and hoped Penny wouldn't snap at him. I watched as he cleared away the straw; he was talking very quietly to her and I couldn't hear what he was saying. He rose to his feet and ran towards the house.

I slipped out from my hiding place. "I think he is alright Penny, don't be afraid of him. I'm sure he is going to help you."

I returned to my hideout as I heard the sound of footsteps. The man reappeared with a woman who was carrying a small bowl. I watched as they knelt down beside Penny. The woman began to stroke her and talk very gently to her as she offered her the contents of the bowl. Penny tried to raise her head but she was too weak. I felt as if I had done the right thing: the humans were being very kind to Penny. The woman gently raised her up so that she could lap from the bowl; she said something to the man who left the barn and went into the house. The woman continued nursing Penny, talking very softly to her. I knew she was in good hands. The man returned shortly with a blanket which he put over my poor friend.

Not long after, a car pulled into the yard. A man got out and came into the barn, carrying a small bag. I could tell at a glance that he was a vet: I had seen a few of them during my time with the circus. He examined Penny very carefully. My heart leapt when I saw him shake his head: I knew what that meant. I watched horrified as he reached into his bag and pulled out a long needle. I closed my eyes as he injected fluid into Penny's vein. I suddenly felt sick as I watched her go limp: once again I felt the tears running down my face as they picked her up and carried her from the barn. The vet carefully put her into the back of his car and drove away. I lay there staring at the pool of blood on the floor; my heart was ready to break. The rain suddenly began to fall, steadily at first, and then it seemed as if the heavens had opened up. I had intended to leave the barn as soon as the humans had gone but changed my mind when I saw what the weather was going to be like. Instead I buried myself in the straw, deciding to stay a while until it cleared up. I must have dozed off, having cried so much. I awoke suddenly as the lightning lit up the sky; it was obvious that the weather was getting worse. I looked around the barn: at least I would be warm and dry if I stayed here. My stomach ached with hunger as I lay there. The sudden cackling of the hen above me brought me to my senses; I crawled out from my hiding place and looked up to where the hen was perched. I guessed she must have had a nest up there, so I began to climb up the bales of straw. My eyes rested on the newly-laid egg. Carefully I touched it with my paw: it was still warm. The hen moved away when she saw me

I suddenly felt very guilty that I was about to steal the egg. The pangs of hunger quickly diminished any sense of guilt. I picked it up and with a little bit of effort managed to climb down to my hiding place. Once on the floor I did what Roger had done – dropping the egg on the floor and cracking it open. I devoured the contents quickly, thinking to myself that it was either steal and survive or starve to death: the former, being a more practical solution to my predicament, quickly confirmed that my actions were justified.

The rain kept on all day and all night. I had hoped that it would have ceased, allowing me to carry on my journey – where to I had no idea: my future seemed somewhat uncertain now that both my friends had gone. I couldn't help feeling responsible for what had happened to Roger and Penny. Despite his ugliness I had become very fond of that boxer but now owing to my stupidity he was dead, and Penny had also suffered because of me. I began to hate myself: everyone I became involved with and cared for were dead except for my two girls whom I thought of very often. I stayed in the barn for two more days and nights, living on stolen eggs. I would sneak out occasionally and drink from the pools of water lying in the yard. It was late in the afternoon of the third day when the rain eventually stopped, much to my relief. I was about to climb up to steal another egg when the car pulled into the yard. I scampered quickly to my hideout and watched as the man got out of the car: it was the vet again. My curiosity was aroused when he opened up the back of the car, I watched as he lifted the dog up. I cannot explain the churning in my stomach as he carried the dog towards the house. I crept forward to get a better view. He withdrew the blanket as he put the dog on the ground: it was Penny, she was alive. My heart leapt with joy as he helped her to her feet. She stood there wrapped in bandages, I felt like running out and giving her a big kiss. She appeared to be a bit wobbly on her legs and had to be supported by the vet. The door of the house opened and out came the woman and the man. They made a great fuss of Penny as she stood there, somewhat dazed. I couldn't believe my eyes. The woman took hold of her and led her into the house. By now I was that excited I wet myself, something I had not done since I was a young girl.

My decision to leave was promptly put aside: how could I go without seeing my dear friend again? Penny who I had given up as dead was alive and in good hands. I waited patiently to see if the humans would bring her out again but as the hours passed by they didn't, so I made up my mind to stay a little longer. After all, there was no rush for me to go. It was early next morning when the humans led Penny into the yards. She appeared to be a lot brighter and tugged on the lead; I could hear the woman laughing as Penny pulled her into the barn. I retreated into the back of the barn and hid myself amongst the bales of straw. I did not want them to find me but Penny insisted on searching the barn: I guessed she knew I was still in hiding. The woman let go of the lead and Penny squeezed herself as near to me as she could. "Po-Po, are you still here?"

I crept forward a little. "Yes Penny I am, but don't give me away. I don't want the humans to know I'm here."

She backed away "I'll see you later then, Po-Po". I smiled as she wormed her way back to where the woman was standing. Penny had lost a lot of weight. I guess she was lucky to be alive.

During the next few days she visited me frequently in the barn. She told me how kind the humans had been to her and how she was becoming attached to them. I knew that it was now time for me to leave.

"Must you go Po-Po?" asked Penny as we lay there chatting.

I think she would have felt much happier if I had said that I would stay, but I knew that the humans would have enough on their hands looking after Penny and it wouldn't be fair on them to find another stray dog in their barn.

"I shall miss you Po-Po," said Penny, wiping a tear from her eye, "you have been the best friend I have ever had."

It was hard for me to leave, but I knew that if I delayed much longer I wouldn't want to leave. I told Penny that I would wait until it was dark before slipping away, she gave me a kiss and wished me well, adding that before I go I must have a good meal. She ran into the house, returning shortly with a big bone with plenty of meat on it.

"I get a lot like that," she said, dropping it at my feet. I told her I was very grateful because by now I was a bit sick of eggs.

"The humans keep calling me Goldie," said Penny, puzzled by it all.

I told her that it was her new name and would please them by answering to it. "Besides, it's a nice name. I like it," I said, looking at her reassuringly.

We could hear the woman calling "Goldie". I nodded to Penny: "Now you must go, my dear. Goodbye and do take care of yourself." She sniffled a bit before she walked away. I could feel the tears building up inside of me as I watched her disappear into the house.

It was a lovely moonlight night and quite warm as I left the farm. I walked down the country lanes for quite a while. It was easy going and very quiet. I had not made any plans at all as to where I was going; I decided just to carry on and see what lay ahead. It would have been very nice if I could have stayed at the farm with Penny but I thought two stray dogs turning up in one place would arouse suspicion, so I knew that there was no choice really. I slept rough most nights and went hungry most of the time I was travelling: I reckoned that was the price I had to pay for getting away from the kennels. It was hard most of the time but occasionally I would manage to sneak around a farm and steal an egg or anything else lying around. I completely lost track of all time as I wandered the countryside aimlessly but enjoying the freedom. By now of course my fur had become quite long: although it kept me warm at night it began to irritate me. I knew that I was in need of clipping but what could I do about it? I couldn't just walk into the nearest town and find a poodle parlour and say, "I would like a clip please." I don't think the humans would have appreciated that.

I lay on the embankment wrapped up in my thoughts. When I heard the rumbling of cartwheels coming down the lane I hid under the hedge as the wagons rolled by. It was an unfamiliar sight to me. Although I had seen wagons before, these were different: they were like little gaily-coloured houses on wheels being drawn along by horses. The humans leading the wagons looked quite scruffy actually and I immediately took an instant dislike to them. Of course, I had never met a gypsy before or even heard of them. Lying hidden away I watched as they passed by.

They didn't appear to be in any hurry; the children were busy picking flowers as they went along and were having a good time. I let them get out of my sight before creeping out into the open again, although I could hear the wheels rumbling along for quite a while afterwards. It began to get dark soon afterwards and I hadn't found anywhere to shelter for the night, so I walked briskly down the lane, hoping that I would come across a farm or a country house that would provide refuge. The nights were getting to be a little cold for sleeping rough, anyway. I preferred the comfort of a warm barn and the sweet smell of straw that I had grown accustomed to.

As I scampered up the embankment and through the hedge I heard the sound of humans laughing somewhere ahead of me. The strong smell of the horses made me realise that I had caught up with the wagons; I hadn't anticipated this as I thought I had given them plenty of time to get ahead of me. I crouched down low and crept forward to investigate. I saw that the lane widened out further on, giving a wide grass verge on which the wagons had parked. The horses had been unhitched and tethered to wooden stakes knocked in the ground and were now quietly grazing whilst the humans went about setting up camp. It reminded me of my days in the circus: there was always a lot of hustle and bustle going on whenever we reached a new town. I lay hidden in the long grass watching the scene below. The humans lit the lanterns in the wagons and started cooking food. My empty stomach turned over as the sweet aroma reached my nostrils: whatever it was certainly smelt delicious. There were four of these brightly painted wagons altogether, spaced out along the verge, two of which had big, mangy-looking Alsatians with them. I counted three altogether plus a little dog, of what breed I could not make my mind up: he looked a bit of all sorts. I reckon his parentage was something of a mystery.

The humans had lit a fire outside the wagons and were gathering round it sitting themselves on the grass smoking and talking. This went on for quite a while. They all seemed to be enjoying themselves; every now and then the air would be filled with laughter. I remained there fascinated by it all. When the rain started the group broke up, disappearing into the wagons. I saw the dogs crawl underneath: apparently they were not allowed inside. The fire was still burning brightly when the door of the third wagon opened. I could just make out the figure of a man: he was throwing something to the dogs. I knew it was food, I could hear them squabbling amongst themselves. It was easy to figure out who would get the biggest share. I had stayed there too long – the rain had become heavier and I was getting very wet, but the smell of food had rooted me to the spot. I decided to wait a while longer in spite of the rain: there was food down there and I needed some. A plan of action began to formulate in my mind, although the sight of those big mangy dogs did give me a cold shiver down my spine.

The rain stopped as I waited patiently for the camp to settle down for the night. I was hoping that the dogs hadn't eaten all the food: maybe they had left a small bone or something, just to take away the hunger pains. The flickering fire gave a warm glow to the camp: it looked so inviting. I was wet, cold and hungry and aching all over. I noticed the dark shadows emerge from beneath the wagon and disappear into the darkness. I guessed the dogs were off on the prowl. It was now or never, I thought to myself as

I circled round the wagons, being careful not to go near the fire. I could smell the meat as I approached the wagon. There was also a strong smell from the dogs where they had been lying; it was obvious that they hadn't had a bath for quite some time. My poor heart was beating vigorously as I crawled under the wagon. I gripped the small bone between my teeth and was about to make my retreat when I saw the dark shape coming towards me. His lips curled back revealing a nasty set of fangs as he lunged at me, snarling viciously. I dropped the bone and jumped upon the axle of the wagon in an effort to avoid the gnashing teeth, it was all I could do to maintain my balance as he crept under the wagon.

I stood there, poised ready for a fight although I knew I would be on the losing end. I bared my teeth defiantly as he approached me.

"What do you think you are doing?" he spat at me.

I stood there looking at the big Alsatian. He reminded me of Jason but he looked a lot meaner.

"I only wanted something to eat," I managed to say, looking him straight in the eye.

"Oh so you're a thief, are you?"

Again his lips curled back, he gave a thunderous bark which almost knocked me off my perch. I thought it was the end for me: I felt sure that at any moment he would tear me to pieces. The door opened and a man appeared, carrying a lantern. He called the dog off as he knelt down and looked under the wagon. A look of surprise crossed his ugly face as he saw me perched on the axle. I don't know who I was afraid of the most, the dog or the man as he reached out for me. I had learned a lot about the humans and knew for sure that if I had bit him it would have been all over for me, so shaking like a leaf I let him pick me up. It was a bit of a struggle for him to manoeuvre under the wagon and I could have slipped from his grasp and made a bolt for it but that mean-looking Alsatian stood there ready to pounce on me.

I was carried into the wagon by the scruff of the neck and dumped onto a table. I looked around at the other humans who appeared to be as surprised as I was. Much to my relief the human closed the door, leaving the Alsatian outside. The wagon, or caravan as they called it, looked very cosy inside and was very warm, but I couldn't stop myself from shaking as I stood there being scrutinized by the occupants. The two young girls gathered round the table and gazed at me as if I had come from another planet. I don't think they had seen a poodle before, especially with my fur clipped the way it was, although I imagine that by now I must have looked a mess. The fat woman looked at me suspiciously and said something to the man about me being on the table: I was immediately placed on the floor. The man examined my collar; I could feel him taking off the metal disc that had my name on it. I struggled as he fumbled with the clasp: it had never been taken off before and I didn't want him to remove it now. His big hands held me firmly as he tried to take the disc off. I growled at him and bared my teeth, only to receive a clip around the ears. Finally he gave up, cursing me for being so stupid. I felt relieved: at least I still had my identity which was worth fighting for.

The man pulled a piece of thick string from his pocket and attached it to my collar to act as a lead. It was quite a let down from the one I had worn in the show ring and I felt rather sad it looked so tatty and not quite what I had been used to. I looked up at the woman as she poured the milk into the saucer. I was famished and began lapping it up before it reached the floor. I was then given some sort of meat which I devoured immediately. The caravan was a bit on the small side. I looked up at the man and wagged my tail, hoping that I would be allowed to sleep inside. The thought of being put outside with the other dogs didn't appeal to me at all. My innocent expression must have melted his heart: I was picked up again and handed to the two girls who immediately made room for me on their bed. I curled up between them and went to sleep.

The humans woke early the following morning and there appeared to be a lot of movement about the camp. I was taken outside by the girls for a little walk which enabled me to relieve myself. I could feel the eyes of the other dogs bearing down upon me as we walked around the caravans. I tensed up as the big Alsatian approached me. The man immediately called him back.

Donovan, as the dog was called, looked at me menacingly. "I'll be seeing you later," he said, staring down at me as if he hated my guts.

I ignored his remark, hoping that I would never be left alone with him. I suppose he was jealous of the attention I was getting from the other humans, which was only natural I suppose, but nevertheless I felt as if I had to watch out for him.

Chapter 8

The men hitched up the horses to the caravans and we set off at a steady pace along the lane. I was left inside but managed to get a good view of the surrounding countryside through one of the windows. Once again I was left alone with my thoughts. I began to wonder about Penny; I knew she would be thinking about me also. It was a pity really that we had to part but after all it was only fair on the humans who had befriended her: one dog was enough to look after. I felt sad as I thought about Roger and hoped that if there was such a thing as a doggies' heaven we would all meet up again one day. I will never forget him though: despite his ugly face he was a real softy at heart. The horses plodded on taking us through small villages and towns. Apparently the gypsies were not very popular with the rest of the humans and we were often called all sorts of names and were always being told to move on. The days passed by; as we travelled on, we always managed to find some quiet place outside of the towns where we would set up camp for maybe a day or so, but we never stayed in one place too long.

Donovan kept an eye on at me all of the time, I knew that one day we would have to have a showdown and sort things out but I wasn't looking forward to it at all: he was the leader of the gang and the other dogs respected him. I saw him have a fight with another Alsatian during our travels and he almost killed the other dog. I'm sure he would have done if the man hadn't parted them. I thought a lot about how I was going to tackle him; most certainly I didn't stand a chance in a fight if ever it came to that, so I had to wrack my brains and devise a plan to win him over as a friend if that was at all possible. The opportunity arose one day as we were camped outside a small village. The humans were going into the village on business and left the caravans except for one man who stayed behind to look after things. I was left inside as usual but the woman had left the window open a little to get rid of the cooking smells. I looked through the window to where Donovan was lying. I plucked up enough courage to call him.

"Can I speak to you for a moment?" I said.

He walked up to the window. "What do you want, thief?" he called out, standing on his hind legs and reaching up to the window.

"You are a good fighter aren't you, Donovan?" I said casually.

He looked at me menacingly. "You had better believe it, sweetheart," he snarled. "Why, do you want a fight?"

I declined the offer, adding that I was very impressed and would like to be able to fight like him. "Would you show me how?" I asked.

He roared with laughter as he looked up at me. "Why, you ain't big enough to bark, let alone fight."

I joined in the laughter, casting an eye over the many scars on his body. He walked away, still laughing: at least I had amused him.

The following day I was being taken for a walk by the two girls when Donovan and the other peculiar dog who they called Heinz walked alongside of us. I kept an eye on Donovan, expecting him to pounce on me at any moment.

"This little kid wants to learn how to fight, Heinz," he said, grinning all over his face,

Heinz burst out laughing, it was obvious they were taking the mickey out of me, but I didn't mind as long as they didn't get aggressive.

"Well, Donovan, maybe we can find a rat or a dead rabbit for her to tussle with," said Heinz sarcastically.

"I did kill a rabbit once," I said proudly, "a big one at that."

Donovan burst out laughing again. "What did you do kid, frighten it to death?"

Heinz joined in the laughter. "I sure would like to have seen that. I bet it was an old woman rabbit," he mused.

"No, as a matter of fact it was quite a young buck rabbit and very strong," I said, ignoring their funny remarks.

"I'd like to see you in action kid," said Donovan, "maybe we will let you tag along when we go hunting and let you have a go. At least it will be a laugh."

I turned and faced him. "I'm going to hold you to that. I'll show you what I'm made of."

Donovan looked down at me. "Of course, it will have to be something very small; we wouldn't expect you to take on anything bigger than yourself. And another thing, you need a haircut."

The fat woman must have thought the same because two days later she picked me up and put me on the table, which was something unusual for her to do. I watched as she picked up the scissors and began snipping away at my fur. I could have told her that the usual procedure was to bath me first then clip me but I don't think for one moment that she had any idea how to go about it. To be quite honest, I felt like a skinned rabbit when she finally finished. Well, I did feel a little cooler when it was all off but if I had entered a show ring looking like I did I'm sure the judge would have laughed his head off. Donovan and the rest of the gang made a few comments when they saw me afterwards but I took no notice of their crude remarks; of course I did have to allow for their upbringing. I was finally allowed to wander about the camp freely without having the piece of string tied to my collar. I was very pleased about this; however, Donovan informed me that I was to stick to my own area as I was not one of the gang.

We moved on again to another place. I lost count how many times we moved altogether but we never stayed for more than a day or two in one particular town. I think it was because we were so unpopular with the other humans. Heinz came up to me one day as the gypsies were busy unhitching the horses. He said that he and the others were off to see what they could find. I decided to follow them at a discreet distance because I knew Donovan would be angry at me for tagging along without being invited. I saw them disappear through the hedge, Donovan in front followed by Kip, the other Alsatian, with Heinz and Rebel close behind. I waited for them to get ahead before I followed. It was impossible to lose them, they gave off such a strong scent; I had to lift my head up time and again because it was so overpowering. They circled around the field looking for rabbit holes. It wasn't long before they found some. Heinz being the smallest tried to crawl down one of them but I could see that he was having a struggle: he was small but a bit on the fat side. Donovan hid in the hedgerow whilst Rebel and the other dog took up their positions nearby. Heinz wasn't having much success I could hear him barking into the hole but it was useless: nothing stirred.

It was pathetic to watch. I could see that there was no way Heinz could get down that hole although he was trying very hard. I decided to make my move: creeping up very slowly, I approached Donovan.

"What are you doing here kid?" he snarled.

I pointed out that Heinz was too fat to get down the hole and that I would be better at it.

"Go on then Poppo, let's see you try," said Donovan angrily.

"My name is Po-Po not Poppo," I said to him firmly, "please try to remember in future" ·

I was amazed at my own audacity and decided to move away before he bit my head off.

Heinz looked up as I nudged him in the side. A look of amazement crossed his face. "What are you doing?" he asked, surprised.

"Step aside Heinz, I'm going down that hole," I said firmly, "you and the others cover the other holes ready for when the fun starts."

Easing myself down on my tummy I began to crawl inside the tunnel. It was very dark inside and I was hoping that it didn't get any smaller as I was having difficulty myself. Leaning my head on one side I listened carefully: I could hear something in front of me moving about. Slowly I inched myself forward a little further. Suddenly I let out a loud bark followed by a loud whine: I made as much noise as I possibly could, hoping that the occupants of the tunnel decided to evacuate the place quickly.

After a little while I began to make my retreat: it was very difficult and I soon began to gasp for air. What a relief it was when I emerged into the fresh air again. I looked around for the others but there was no sign of them. Suddenly I heard a loud squeal from further along the hedge. I ran to investigate, knowing that it didn't sound like a rabbit. Rebel appeared from nowhere, followed by Heinz; they looked worried as we raced along.

"That sounded like Donovan," panted Heinz.

Rebel was the first to arrive on the scene. He stopped in his tracks and stood there gaping as Donovan struggled with the wire around his neck. I was out of breath when I reached them and was unable to speak for a moment. Dinkie had told me all about snares and how cruel they were. We had seen a rabbit caught in one once and it horrified me to see the poor thing strangle itself trying to get out of it. I knew I had to act fast in order to prevent Donovan doing the same.

"Don't move, lie perfectly still," I shouted, but he was fighting for his life and didn't hear me.

I called to Rebel and Heinz to help but they just stood there as if in a trance. I nipped Rebel on the leg to get his attention. "Tell Donovan to lie still or he will be dead in no time. Hurry Rebel, there's no time to lose".

He lay down beside Donovan whose eyes were almost bulging out of his head as he pulled at the wire. He shouted at Donovan to lie still. I looked at the wire buried deep into his neck. I called to Heinz as I followed the wire to where it was fastened to the wooden stake buried deep in the earth.

"We have got to dig around this and try to get it out of the ground," I yelled, digging furiously.

"Let me help," said a voice behind me. I turned to see the other dog standing there. He was a big dog with very powerful-looking paws. I stood back as the black Labrador's legs worked away, moving the earth around the stake. Finally he took hold with his jaws and pulled at it, tearing it from the ground. I looked at Donovan: he began to pant heavily as the wire eased around his neck. I held the wire in my teeth and gently slipped it over his head. We stood there watching and waiting as he eventually regained consciousness, his neck soaked with blood where the wire had cut into him.

It was days later before Donovan recovered from his ordeal, I don't think he will ever forget how near to death he was. We were following the caravans down a country lane when he came alongside of me. "I owe you my life Po-Po, the others told me how well you handled the situation. I want you to know how grateful I am."

I told him it was nothing. "I'm sure you would have done the same for me," I said casually.

He looked down at me with his big eyes. "You are one of the gang now Po-Po, and if ever you need anything just let me know.'

I thanked him for being so kind. I felt very proud of being accepted into the pack and the other dogs treated me with great respect. We reached the camp early in the afternoon. I was surprised to see all the other caravans gathered together on the piece of waste ground; there were quite a number of them and lots of other gypsies. I asked Donovan what they were all doing there as I had no idea what was happening.

"This is our annual get together," he said, staying close to me as we wandered through the rows of caravans, "we meet up with all our old friends and there's a lot of trading goes on. It's good fun Po-Po, but stay close to me as there are some very rough characters around."

I was very amused by all the goings on, especially with the horse-trading: the gypsies showed off their prize animals and some heavy bargaining went on. Occasionally some of the gypsies got into fights. It was fun to watch them knocking each other about. Donovan explained that all accounts were settled at the annual meet but when it was all over everyone appeared to be friends again.

The two girls took me for a stroll one day and as we were passing one of the caravans a nasty-looking dog appeared and began to show a great interest in me. I tried to ignore him but he was very persistent and followed us all the way back to our camp. I saw Donovan eyeing him suspiciously as we drew near to our caravan.

"I think you had better get yourself lost now," I said to the stranger, but he ignored my remark. The next thing I knew Donovan had him by the throat and I'm sure he would have killed him if I hadn't butted in.

He let go of the dog who was very badly shaken "Perhaps you will do as the lady says next time," said Donovan, standing between me and the dog.

The stranger walked away, I turned to Donovan who was keeping a watchful eye on him. "Thank you very much," I said, gazing up at him.

"That's alright Po-Po, I'll stand up for you any time."

I smiled at him. "I don't mean for fighting over me, I meant for calling me a lady."

He coloured up a little. "Well you are Po-Po, compared to some of these other females."

We moved on again after a few days, leaving the other gypsies to go their own ways. It had been fun and I had enjoyed myself. I realised that I was getting used to this way of life; certainly there was plenty of freedom and I wasn't short of friends now. The one thing that puzzled me most was why it was always the eldest of the girls who always spoke to me. The younger one never spoke at all: she only made signs with her hands which I could never understand. I decided to ask Heinz about her.

"She can't speak, Po-Po," he said, "she can only make signs."

This puzzled me even more "But all humans can speak," I replied.

Heinz shook his head. I found it hard to believe and also very sad. I decided to be more friendly towards her: if anyone needed a friend it was this poor little girl. When we set up our next camp I took hold of my 'lead' and held it up to her, she seemed to understand and followed me outside.

I tugged on the lead playfully, watching her eyes light up. I knew she enjoyed playing with me but we had never been allowed to play alone. Her sister had always accompanied us, but she was having her hair washed in the caravan. I rolled over on the grass allowing her to tickle my tummy. I could see how thrilled she was, so I thought I would show off a bit and began to do some of my circus tricks. Her mouth opened to laugh but no sound came out, I gave a little bark and looked up at her but she made no sound; she only opened her mouth again and looked down at me. She became very excited as I stood on my hind legs and pirouetted two or three times. Again I stood in front of her and barked; I saw her trying to copy me but there was still no sound coming from her. A couple of forward somersaults amused her. I could see she was getting very excited so I continued with a reverse roll and a backward flip. I looked up at her again and gave a loud whine. She tried to copy me again but still no sound came; I repeated this action, watching her forming her lips. Raising my head back I whined again; she did the same but this time I heard a slight sound from the back of her throat. I knew she was trying very hard to copy me. What it needed was a little more practice.

I hadn't noticed but the gypsy woman had been watching us from the caravan. I heard her approach us from behind; she knelt down beside the girl and put her arm around her. I raised my head back again and whined. The girl tried to copy me and the gypsy woman seemed very excited. She put her head back and made a sound something like I had done. The little girl tried again: this time the sound was a little bit stronger. The woman became very excited and encouraged the girl to do it again. After several more attempts the girl had mastered it and kept on doing it, I reckon it must have been the first time in her life she had made a sound and she was very thrilled about it so was I. Michele always made me do my tricks over and over again until I had got them right and I think this was how it was going to be with this little girl. I had to get her to keep trying. I lifted my head again and let out a little howl; watching the girl trying to copy me, it was all so funny really. The gypsy woman must have known what I was doing and imitated the sound I made. I can't imagine what the others must have thought as they watched us making those funny noises. Rosy, the little girl, put her head back and tried to howl but nothing came out, I did it again and so did the woman. We watched as Rosy tried to copy us: she was trying very hard and after a while much to our surprise out it came. The gypsy woman hugged her with delight, she ran and fetched the man who wondered what all the excitement was about. He sat down on the grass with us: a look of amazement crossed his face when Rosy lifted her head back and howled.

From that day on the humans began to encourage Rosy to make further sounds. I felt as if I had done my part so I left them to it. Several days later as we were travelling along the road I happened to be lying on Rosy's bed with her, it was raining so I stayed in the caravan on that particular day. Rosy was playing with me and making all kinds of sounds. Suddenly I heard her say my name: although it didn't quite sound right it was something like it. I looked at her and barked with excitement. She repeated it several times; eventually she pronounced it right. I was overwhelmed with joy. The humans must have been helping her and now after all those years of silence here she was beginning to talk. It was a very touching moment. As the days passed by Rosy, with the help of her parents, managed to say other words; although I could not understand them her parents could. Donovan said I had magical powers but I didn't think that at all. It was just a matter of practising, like any other trick.

I don't know why it was, but wherever we went we were always visited by some humans in uniforms, they would come to our camp in their cars with a blue light flashing all the time and there would be arguments between them and the gypsies. Donovan and the rest of the gang would stand there in front of them with lips curled back ready to pounce. I don't know why they made such a fuss. The gypsies never hurt anyone, but there it was: for some reason beyond my understanding we were never welcome anywhere. Anyway I didn't take any notice of them, I thought it best to keep my nose out of it. Well, I decided to stay with them. I was enjoying the carefree way of life. It certainly was better than being in the kennels; I was fed regularly and treated with great respect by the gypsies. I feel sure that Roger would have loved this life if he had lived.

Chapter 9

We moved on again to another town. It was early in the morning as we passed through; it was raining again so once more I stayed in the caravan. I stared hard at the iron railings surrounding the park. There was something very familiar about; it was as if I had been there before. I looked at them at them again.

As the caravans slowly passed by suddenly it came to me: this was the town I had lived in with Mary and her family and that was the park where they used to take me for walks. Those happy days which seemed a long time ago flashed through my mind, bringing back many memories that would remain there forever. I couldn't help feeling unhappy as we left the park behind. We set up camp outside the town on a piece of waste ground. I wished we had moved on to somewhere else; I felt very depressed at being so near to the place where I had once lived, being reminded of the wonderful family who had given me a home.

We had been there two days before the "blue bellies", as Donovan called them, came to visit us. It was the same old problem: we were not allowed to stay there. I watched as the gypsies argued with the men in uniforms.

Donovan rounded up the gang. "I feel like a fight," he said, looking at us. "Let's give them blue bellies something to remember us by."

I asked him what he had in mind: not that I was in the mood for fighting, but being a member of the gang I had to follow orders. I knew Donovan was spoiling for action as he hadn't had a fight for ages.

The others listened as he laid out his plan. "We don't want to get into too much trouble, do we, so let's just scare them off a bit.

Po-Po, you just grab hold of one of them by his trouser leg and rip it to bits. Rebel and I will keep an eye on you, if they touch you we will go for them. Heinz, you get under their feet and trip them up, the other two can stand by in case we need reinforcements. That clear to you all?"

We moved in slowly. I felt very nervous as I approached one of the blue bellies. I could see that he was busy writing something down in a book and did not notice me creep up on him. I grabbed hold of his trouser leg and pulled at it; it tasted horrible but I held on and kept pulling, waiting to see what was going to happen. He looked down at me and laughed his head off. I felt very hurt and growled at him; again I tugged at the material, hoping it would tear.

Well I'm only seven inches tall and my mouth isn't very big so I don't know what damage Donovan expected me to do to the blue bellies' trousers, the material was very tough and wouldn't tear. I felt a sharp clip around the ears as he bent down and struck at me. Donovan moved in, leaping up at him; Heinz slipped between his legs, tripping him up. I felt sorry for the blue belly lying there with Donovan snarling at him. The other blue belly stepped back; I could see that he was frightened by the sudden attack and did nothing to help his companion. The rest of the gang closed in, forming a circle around them. I couldn't help myself, I ran up to the blue belly lying on the ground and licked his face. He looked at me with surprise: I bet he thought I was going to tear him to bits. The gypsies called us off. I could see they were laughing their heads off at our little escapade. It had been a bit of harmless fun and I think the blue bellies took it in good humour.

Donovan was still laughing as we returned to the caravan. "What on earth happened Po-Po, why didn't you rip his pants?"

I shook my head. "The material was too tough for me, and besides it tasted horrible. You can do it next time, you have got a better grip than me."

We watched as the blue bellies got into their car and left.

It was late in the afternoon of the following day. We were prowling round the fields looking for rabbits, all except Heinz who was 'too tired' to hunt. We hadn't been out long when Heinz came chasing after us; he seemed very excited about something as he ran towards us.

"Changed your mind then?" said Donovan as Heinz lay there panting.

"No, it's the blue bellies. They have come back again," he gasped.

Donovan looked at him. I noticed the mischievous look in his eye. "Have they brought any blue belly dogs with them?" he asked.

Heinz shook his head. "No, but there is another human with them, but I don't think he's a blue belly."

Donovan looked disappointed. "That's a pity. I fancied having a go at a blue belly dog, they say they are very good fighters and I wanted to find out if it was true. Anyway, let's go and see what they are up to."

We crept into the camp and hid under one of the caravans. "Right, we will wait and see if there's going to be any aggro before we make our move," said Donovan, eyeing up the blue bellies. "I don't know who that one is in the white raincoat but he must be something to do with them. Now listen, if they start shouting at the gypsies or show any signs of aggravation we will rush out and circle them, but don't attack unless I give the word. Po-Po, you take the one in the mac and the rest of us will go for the blue bellies. Have you all got that?"

We nodded our heads. I couldn't see the human's face who was to be my target as he was standing with his back towards me but it did not matter: I could sneak up behind him unnoticed and grab his leg. We could hear the humans talking very loudly to each other: the blue bellies were showing the gypsies some papers and kept pointing to them. The gypsies became angry. I could sense the trouble that was coming.

"Right, circle round them," said Donovan, leading off.

I made straight for the human with the mac on; he didn't notice me standing behind him ready to pounce. I saw Donovan and the others moving into position.

By now the humans were shouting at each other. I decided to liven things up a bit by grabbing at the man's trouser leg and pulling at it, hoping to tear a piece out. I felt him lash out at me with his foot but I moved away quickly and he missed. Again I made a grab at him. It was then that his scent reached me: a strange feeling came over me as I stood there, rooted to the spot. There was something familiar about his scent. His hand came out of his pocket: it was then I saw the burn marks. I moved closer to him and sniffed his scent. He turned round and looked down at me. I thought I was going to pass out: it was Mary's father. He smiled at me and bent down, holding out the back of his hand for me either to bite or lick, I wasn't sure. I could see the scars on the side of his neck; they looked very nasty. I licked the back of his hand and wagged my tail. I suddenly found myself getting very excited and jumped up to him, barking like mad with joy. I could hear Donovan calling me but I took no notice; I was completely out of this world with excitement. Mary's father stood up and turned away from me, much to my surprise. I couldn't understand why he had not recognised me.

"What's the matter with you?" asked Donovan, running up to me.

I looked at him mystified. "He doesn't know who I am," I said.

"What are you talking about?" said Donovan, looking at me as if I were mad.

"It's my owner but he doesn't know me," I blurted out.

The big dog looked down at me. "What are you saying Po-Po? I thought you told us that they were all killed in that crash. Are you sure? Some of these humans all look alike at times."

I sniffed around the man again. There was no doubt about it. His scent was strong and he had handled me enough times for me not to forget. "Yes Donovan I am sure, but what can I do? He doesn't know me."

I saw Donovan's face drop into a sad expression. "You know what would happen if he knew, Po-Po? He would take you away from us. Would you want that?"

I was all mixed up inside, it was a decision only I could make. "I don't know Donovan, I'm all confused. You have all been so kind to me and such good friends."

He looked down at me with his sad eyes. "It's up to you, Po-Po. No one can make your mind up for you but I don't mind saying that if you go we will all miss you terribly. You have become more than a friend to me and I owe you my life."

I could feel the tears coming into my eyes, it was a very difficult decision to make. I had become so fond of Donovan and the rest of the gang and I was enjoying my freedom.

"You don't know for sure if he would want you back anyway," said Donovan. This hadn't occurred to me: maybe I was getting all upset about nothing. After all, it had been such a long time ago and besides, how could I get him to recognise me after all this time?

The rest of the gang were looking at us wondering what was going on. I watched Donovan walk over to where they were standing. I could see that he was explaining the situation to them. The man bent down again and started to stroke my head. That did it, I jumped up and licked his hand and began barking my head off. Rosy came out of the caravan and came over; she reached out for me but I darted round her. I couldn't risk being taken away from Mary's father yet without him knowing who I was. Rosy became very angry as she chased after me; I darted in between his feet and looked up at him. He seemed to be very amused by it all. Rosy called my name. I saw the puzzled expression on his face as he looked down at me. He said something to Rosy, but she didn't answer. She ran and stood beside her mother who was joining in with the other gypsies arguing with the blue bellies. He bent down and called my name, I ran up to him barking and wagging my tail. I'm afraid I wet myself again with all the excitement. Picking me up he ran his fingers through my collar and looked at the disc. A look of surprise crossed his face as he stared at it.

"Po-Po," he said, hugging me to him and ruffling my fur.

Well I couldn't help wetting myself again; he laughed as he shook his hand. Donovan and the others looked on. I couldn't help but detect the sad look in their eyes as Mary's father stepped forward and interrupted the blue bellies who were still arguing it out with the gypsies. I suddenly found that I now became the centre of attraction as Mary's father exchanged words with Rosy's mother and father. A lot of talking went on: Rosy began crying and her mother reached out for me. I bared my teeth at her defiantly.

The arguing carried on for quite some time. I couldn't understand what was going on but Mary's father kept pointing to my collar and the disc attached to it.

Donovan walked up and looked at me. "You've caused a lot of trouble I'm afraid Po-Po, but I reckon you have made your own mind up, haven't you?'

I looked down at him sadly. "Yes Donovan, I must go. I'm sure you understand, don't you?"

He shook his head. "We are all going to miss you Po-Po, but if that's what you want then we won't make any trouble. I've spoken to the rest of the gang and I'm sure they feel the same way as I do."

I was deeply touched by his sentiment. I could feel the tears welling up in my eyes again. "I'm going to miss you all very much Donovan, you know that, don't you?"

I saw the tears running down his face. I hadn't seen him cry before and it brought a lump into my throat. That vicious-looking dog had a soft spot after all. Finally the humans stopped arguing amongst themselves. I felt Mary's father put his hand into his pocket and pull out his wallet. I saw him give Rosy's mother a handful of paper money which she grabbed, uttering a lot of angry words. I felt sorry for Rosy: she was crying bitterly. I knew she was very fond of me and I was of her.

I heard the gang calling out to me as I was carried towards the car, "Look out for us Po-Po, we'll be passing this way again."

The tears were streaming down my face as I looked out through the rear window of the car. I hoped I would see them again some time; they had been such good companions and I knew I would miss them. The other business of the gypsies seemed to have been forgotten. I suddenly became the centre of attraction in the car. I had no idea that blue bellies could be so friendly. The jolting of the car made me sick and I made a right mess of his mac, but Mary's father didn't seem to mind this time. I recognised the house as the car pulled up outside: it hadn't changed any since I was last there. Heaven knows how long that had been. Mary's father got out of the car and the blue bellies drove off after giving me a bit of fuss.

Chapter 10

I heard a dog bark as we entered the house. My heart sank: I didn't know that I had been replaced. I suddenly became very sad at the thought of another dog taking my place. As Mary's father opened the door to the living room a small white thing rushed out to greet him. I looked down at the poodle dancing around his feet. Mary's father placed me down on the floor: I stood facing the dog who was living in my home. He was small, maybe an inch taller than myself but no more. He looked at me in amazement. I suppose he was wondering what on earth I was; I hadn't had a bath for ages and my fur looked a proper mess. I couldn't help notice how well-groomed he was and felt very embarrassed at my own appearance. I must have looked like a scrubbing brush to him.

"Er, hello," he said politely with a look of uncertainty in his eye. "I'm Toby, I live here."

I tried to hide my embarrassment by being tough: "Oh yes, well I'm Po-Po and I lived here before you."

We stood there looking at each other; I must admit he was a good looking dog and very polite. I walked into the living room: nothing had changed it was exactly how I had remembered it.

Toby watched as I looked the place over, "Would you like a drink or something?" he asked, pointing to the water in the bowl. I noticed his nose twitching as he lay down on the mat. I knew what it was: I could smell myself and believe me, it was quite strong.

"I think I would like a nice bath most of all," I replied apologetically. "I know, I smell don't I?"

He smiled at me then broke into a broad grin. "Yes you do pong a bit, but I don't suppose you can be blamed for that."

I told him that I had been living rough for some time and had not had a bath or been clipped properly for I didn't know how long.

He shrugged his shoulders. "Well I'm sure Mary and her mother will see to that when they come home."

I stared at him. "Do you mean they are all right, they are not dead?"

Toby shook his head. "No Po-Po, they are all right except for some minor burns. I believe they thought you were dead though or else I wouldn't be here, would I?"

My feelings towards Toby began to change. He was being very kind and understanding; it was me who had been rude to him, so I apologised.

"There's no need for that Po-Po, I can see that you have suffered quite considerably," he said in a gentle tone.

The door opened and in rushed Mary, followed by her mother. I was picked up hugged and kissed by them both; it was a lovely feeling to be home again. Mary's mother said something to her and I was whisked away to the bathroom where I bathed in lovely warm water. it was to feel the warm air drying my fur. I couldn't help notice how black the water looked as Mary pulled out the plug in the wash basin. My fur was all knotted up and Mary had difficulty in brushing it; she said something to her mother who nodded her head in agreement. They finished drying me off and took me back downstairs. Toby was there waiting.

"My word Po-Po, what a difference there is and hmm you do smell nice."

I thanked him for his compliment, adding that I only needed a good clipping and I would feel more like a toy poodle again. It was hard to realise that I was back home after all this time. I lay awake all that night unable to believe that it was all so real. So much had happened to me. I began to cry for some reason; whether it was because was so happy or because I missed my friends I don't know. Toby snuggled up to me. He reminded me of Dinkie in a way: so kind and understanding,

"You can tell me all about it if you wish Po-Po. Maybe it will help," he whispered.

He listened as I began to tell him of my adventures; he never interrupted as I rambled on and on. I think I must have kept him awake all night but he didn't mind.

"You certainly have seen something of the world, Po-Po," he said after I had finished talking, "but it's all in the past now – you are home and you must try and forget all that's happened."

I told him that I would never be able to forget those who had befriended me during my travels, and especially my two little girls who I had to leave behind.

"Well maybe one day the circus will come to our town, you never know Po-Po. I know that sometimes they have fairs and such things in town because Mary took me with her to one of them, but I didn't like all the noise and such. I was very frightened of those dreadful machines the humans like to go on."

Toby was such a comfort to me. I listened as he told me how he had been brought home as a pet for Mary. "She didn't like me at first. I think she missed you very much. I've heard your name mentioned so many times since I've been here, so I don't think they ever forgot you, Po-Po."

The following morning I was taken to the Poodle Parlour and given the full treatment – it felt so good! Toby said how beautiful I looked when we returned to the house. I thanked him for his compliments, adding that he was rather attractive himself, which of course made him blush a little. We got on very well together which pleased the humans very much and I suppose it was inevitable that Toby and I should start a family of our own. Several months passed by, the winter came and covered the ground with snow. I wondered how Donovan and the gypsies managed when it was like this.

It was early spring when I noticed the slight movement inside of me; I told Toby who jumped for joy at the news that he was going to be a father. "But you know that the humans won't let you keep them," he said sadly. It was rather a sad thought but I didn't mind as long as they went to good homes.

I don't know why it is but my children always seem to choose the wrong moment to make their appearance in this world. It was during the early hours of the morning when I began to feel unwell. I became very thirsty and was panting heavily; when Toby appeared at my side he seemed rather concerned.

"Is there anything I can do, Po-Po?" he asked kindly,

I said he could have the babies for me if he wished and tried to laugh at my own humour but I was in terrible pain and couldn't raise a smile. After some time I realised that something wasn't going right. It had been difficult before with my other two, but this time it was really hard and Michele wasn't around to help me. I lay there panting, wondering what to do. Toby must have realised something was wrong and began to bark his head off. I felt relieved a little when the light was switched on and Mary's father appeared in the room. he looked at me and then fetched Mary's mother. I began to cry out as the pain got worse; I knew something was wrong and I needed help. The cool water Mary's mother brought eased the burning in my throat but the pain only increased. I heard the humans talking amongst themselves, Mary's father left the room and I heard him talking to someone on the telephone. After what seemed an eternity the vet arrived; he took a look at me and then began feeling my body. I felt the needle being pushed into me but that was nothing compared to what I was going through. I must have passed out; I don't remember anything after that. As I began to regain consciousness I could feel the two little creatures nibbling at my tummy; I knew it was all over. The humans stood looking down at me as I lay there with my children. They put out the lights and went back to bed leaving me somewhat in the dark in more ways than one. Toby sneaked out from beneath the settee and lay down beside me.

I spoke quietly to him. "Toby I don't think I could go through all that again," I said feeling very glad that it was all over. 'It was easier last time and I didn't have the vet to help me, so something must have gone wrong."

He gave a deep sigh. "Yes Po-Po, I was very worried. I thought for a moment you were going to die. I heard the vet say something about the babies being the wrong way and it frightened me, so I hid under the settee until it was all over. I am a coward, aren't I?"

I gave a little laugh; at least he was honest. I must have been exhausted because I fell asleep while Toby was still talking to me. When I awoke Toby was standing beside me looking at the babies who were fast asleep.

"Aren't they beautiful Po-Po, isn't it marvellous?" I looked at him: he was as proud as punch.

"A boy and a girl," I laughed, "what a change that makes."

The humans were very excited about the whole event when they came down and made such a fuss of me and the babies. I felt sorry for Toby: nobody seemed to pay any attention to him and he looked quite hurt about it.

"Never mind Toby, you can have them next time and all the glory will be yours," I said to him afterwards. He laughed at me, adding that he had contributed in a small way.

We had a lot of fun with the babies and as they began to feel their feet they began to get up to all kinds of mischief and there was many a day when I was glad to see them settled down for the night.

"Do you think they look like you and me?" asked Toby one evening as we lay there. I laughed my head off; he was very funny at times.

"Well if they looked like that tomcat next door I would be worried," I said, looking at them as they snuggled up together in the basket. "Of course they look like us, silly."

I remarked that I was glad I was a poodle and not a boxer. "They are really ugly," I said, "but very friendly," I added, thinking of Roger again and how much I had loved him.

Toby said that it was such a shame we weren't allowed to keep them. "The humans don't give their babies away, do they Po-Po?"

I knew how he felt. I had been through it all before and knew how sad we would be when the time came. "I don't mind Toby as long as they go to some nice family like ours, I would feel different if they ended up in a kennels or some other place where they weren't treated as pets."

When the time did arrive for our children to be taken away I was relieved to find out that they were going to some relatives of Mary's. I told Toby that we had nothing to worry about and that we would probably see them quite often, he was pleased to hear that. In fact we did see them at regular intervals and were very pleased to see that they grew up to be very nice dogs; that in itself was something. We settled down again to a normal life enjoying our walks in the park and going on holidays. I was glad I had decided not to stay with the gypsies; it was so much better having a permanent home, although every now and then I would find myself day-dreaming about hunting rabbits in the open fields. I tried to forget about the kennels and the show ring, that hadn't been much fun although it had been an experience.

Quite some time later Mary took us to the Poodle Parlour for our usual clipping but instead of going in the car, for some unknown reason we had to go by bus. As we were walking along the street I noticed a human sticking some brightly coloured papers on a wall.

I dug in my heels as I watched him unfold them. "What's the matter, Po-Po?" asked Toby, taken by surprise by my action.

"It's a circus," I cried out excitedly as I studied the picture pasted on the wall. "Look Toby, can you see those poodles in the ring?"

My heart was in my mouth as Mary tried to coax me along. I pretended I wanted to relieve myself and squatted down. Mary seemed very cross but I wasn't bothered: my eyes were glued on the pictures. I knew it was my girls in the picture, there was no doubt about it.

"Come on Po-Po," called out Toby, "Mary's very cross with you." I ran along wagging my tail I was very excited and did a couple of pirouettes which brought a look of astonishment to Toby's face.

"Have you gone bonkers?" he asked as I calmed down.

When we returned home I began to ask Toby where the humans took him when they went to the fair. I knew that usually a piece of ground was kept available for such events

"I'm not sure Po-Po, but I don't think it was very far: we walked it."

I begged him to try and remember, stressing how important it was to me. I knew that I had to see Cindy and Candy again; I was so glad Mitzi had told me about the posters. Toby said he would try and find out where it was, seeing how determined I was, but remarked that he couldn't see us being taken to a circus. I told him to leave everything to me: if I could mastermind an escape from a kennels I'm damn well sure I could arrange a little night excursion to a circus "Hmph, Toby must think I'm thick," I said to myself.

When Mary took us out for our walks Toby pointed out that they had gone in the opposite direction on the night she had taken him to the fair.

"Right then," I said, "pull hard on your lead and let's go that way."

Mary was very cross with us as we turned and pulled her along. I felt sorry really behaving so badly, but it had to be done.

"This way, I think," said Toby as we turned the corner. Finally Mary let us have our way and followed, but very reluctantly. Toby stopped and looked at me: "I think we went down here."

I pulled on the lead, heading in the direction. At last we came to a large field on the edge of the town. It hadn't been all that far away and I knew that I could remember where it was.

"There's nothing there, Po-Po," remarked Toby, looking into the field, "I'm sure this is the place alright".

Mary was very cross with us both when we returned home and shut us in the house. "Now see what you have done," said Toby, very annoyed.

I told him not to worry as we would be forgiven later on when she had cooled down a bit. "Anyway it does you good to go somewhere else for a change," I replied triumphantly.

I knew that it wouldn't be long before the circus came to town and began to make plans. If we persisted enough when we were taken for our walks I knew that Mary would eventually give in to us, humans being what they are. I asked Toby to play along with me each time we went out and eventually we won: we were taken into the field and allowed to run around. One evening as we were being led home I saw the huge wagons carrying all the circus things heading towards the field.

"There you are Toby, I told you, didn't I?"

He looked at me. "Yes you did, but how are we going to get out of the house and go there?" he asked.

I told him that I had it all planned out in my head. "You should have been a brain surgeon," he replied indignantly.

That evening when the family went to bed I showed Toby what I could do by pushing the stool near to the door, and placing my paw on the handle I opened it.

"That's easy but what about the other one? That's locked."

I led him into the place where all the food was cooked and pointed to the wash basin. "Could you jump up onto there if I fetched the stool?" I asked him.

He looked at me as if I were daft. "Yes I could if I wanted to," came the reply.

"Good, that's all I wanted to know, now if you want you can come with me but I won't mind if you don't want to."

He shook his head and heaved a deep sigh. "I don't know Po-Po, what happens if we get caught?"

I told him not to worry as we were not going just yet. "We will wait until the family go out one of these evenings or when they go to bed. Leave it to me Toby, I'm a master at this sort of thing."

Poor Toby, I bet he thought I was a nut case. "Are you sure you can open that window?" he asked as we lay on the mat.

"A piece of cake to someone like me," I replied, winking my eye at him. "Well, wouldn't you want to see your children if you hadn't seen them for ages?" I said, putting on an angry tone. He nodded his head. "I knew you would understand. Toby that's why I think you are the greatest."

I seemed to have won him over. "Do you really think that about me, Po-Po?" he asked curiously.

"Why of course I do, Toby darling," I replied, licking his ear.

He smiled at me affectionately. I knew I could rely on him: well we do have our ways of getting what we want. I decided that the best time to visit the circus would be when the family had gone to bed for the night. Everywhere would be nice and quiet and we wouldn't have to rush back. I told Toby this and he agreed. The only problem would be getting back into the house: it was quite a jump up to the kitchen from outside, so I knew we would have to have something handy to stand on. The following day we scoured the garden for some suitable object that we could easily move into position.

"Will this do?" asked Toby, leaping onto a wooden box behind the shed.

"It will if we can move it," I replied, placing my front paws and pushing it. Toby helped me and between us we managed to roll it over onto its side.

"Yes I think that will do fine, only we need to get it near to the house so that we don't have to move it too far on the night we go out."

Toby looked at me. "Have you decided when to go?" he asked.

"Yes, tomorrow night when they are all in bed."

The following day we played in the garden with the box gradually pushing it towards the house.

"That will be all right Toby let's leave it there and hope the humans don't move it away." I was very pleased with my plan and couldn't wait to put it into action, I wanted so much to see my daughters.

We waited patiently for the family to go to bed, it seemed endless just lying there waiting but finally the light was put out and off they went.

"Let's give them a little time to settle down," I suggested to Toby who was anxious to get it over with; he was very restless and couldn't settle down. "You have to learn to be patient," I said, watching him pace up and down, "I can't help feeling a bit nervous Po-Po, I've never done anything like this before," I reassured him that all would be well if he kept his cool and followed me.

There was no difficulty in getting out of the house, everything went according to plan and we managed to place the box beneath the window without disturbing anyone in the house. I was very excited as we walked down the street towards the field, it was all I could do to prevent myself from racing ahead of Toby but we had to play safe and not arouse any suspicion, not that there were many humans about at that time of night.

We slipped through the gate into the field, "How will you know where they are?" asked Toby looking at all the tents and trailers.

"Follow my nose of course," I said excitedly.

We worked our way around the circus perimeter, it was difficult in the dark to tell which tent was which, so I had to rely on my sense of smell, I recognised some of the familiar scents as we crept cautiously amongst the tents. The big top was easy to recognise so I thought I would take Toby inside to have a look.

"Is this where you used to perform Po-Po, in here?"

I told him that I had spent many hours under the big top and had enjoyed every moment of it, that is until that horrible human with the fire sticks had ruined my career.

Leaving the big top we made our way towards a familiar looking tent, I recognised it because it was a different shape to the others. "This is it Toby," I whispered, "You stay here while I sneak in and see if it is all clear."

He looked at me nervously, "Don't be long Po-Po, I wouldn't know what to do if someone came and found me here." I crept inside hoping that Michele still kept the dogs in here, as usual there was a small light hanging from the centre pole, it wasn't very bright but was enough for me to see that I had chosen the right tent, the dogs were all sleeping in their boxes. I sniffed my way around until I detected my old friend. My poor heart was thumping like a big drum as I gently nudged her.

"Psst, Mitzi, wake up Mitzi."

She stirred and lifted up her head, "What is it, who are you?" she asked half asleep.

I nudged her again. "Mitzi, it's me Po-Po."

She sniffed me suspiciously. "Po-Po, is it really you Po-Po?"

Even in the dim light I could see that there was something wrong with her. "What's the matter Mitzi, don't you recognise your old friend?" I looked at her, I could see that her eyes were glazed over, poor Mitzi my dear old friend, she was blind, I could have cried.

I licked her face all over.

"I'm so glad to see you again Po-Po, I've thought of you often. I hoped some day you would find us." She stumbled blindly from her box.

"What has happened to your eyes, Mitzi?" I asked.

She wept a little. "I made the same mistake as you Po-Po, I tried to make friends with the fire eater and this is what he did to me."

As I looked at her I could feel my stomach turning over: how could a human be so cruel as to do that? I rubbed my nose against her affectionately. "Didn't Michele do anything about it?" I asked.

Mitzi nodded her head. "Yes, the man was dismissed from the circus immediately but the damage was done, wasn't it?"

It was a sad sight to see, I felt very sorry for her. "Are my girls still with the circus, Mitzi?"

She nodded her head. "Yes, they are in the nursery."

I looked at her. "In the what?"

She began to walk slowly towards the exit of the tent. "Oh, I forgot you wouldn't know, would you? They both have babies now. Follow me Po-Po and I'll take you to them."

I was flabbergasted. I had forgotten how old my girls were. "My goodness Mitzi, what a delightful surprise. That makes me a grandmother, doesn't it?"

She told me that they both had given birth more or less at the same time. "You will like the babies Po-Po, and your girls are very good mothers."

I followed her into another tent which was dimly lit by a single bulb. I peered into the first box: Cindy was curled up inside with two beautiful white puppies beside her. Candy looked up as I approached her box, I could see she was nursing two little bundles.

Her eyes lit up as she recognised me. "Mama, is that really you?"

I smiled at her. "Yes my darling, it's your Mama come to see you."

She grew very excited. I told her to calm down and let me see her babies. They were very beautiful I couldn't help thinking how it was when I brought my first babies into the world.

"You must be very proud of them Candy, they both look like you."

Cindy poked her head out of her box and looked at me. "Mama, oh Mama how nice to see you again! Look Mama, have you seen our babies?"

It was a very touching moment: my little girls were all grown up with babies of their own. I couldn't help the tears of joy streaming down my face as I looked at my family.

Mitzi nudged me gently. "I think there's someone outside, Po-Po." I had forgotten all about Toby.

"It's alright Mitzi, it's my husband Toby. I had forgotten all about him."

We all sat looking at each other. It was a moment I shall always remember and treasure. Toby nudged me gently in the side. "It's starting to get light Po-Po, don't you think we should be getting back now?"

We had been there for a long time: how the time had fled. We had been talking for hours. Mitzi had fallen asleep; she was getting old now. We said our farewells to Candy and Cindy. I found it very difficult to tear myself away from them.

"Don't wake Mitzi up, let her sleep and promise me you will take good care of her as she has done for you."

They began to cry as we turned to leave: I couldn't help going back and making a fuss of them.

"Shall we see you again, Mama?" they asked.

I told them that we would always look out for the circus and visit them whenever they came to our town. I kissed them both and followed Toby out of the tent. We had to hurry home before the humans got up.

I looked at Toby as we lay on the mat, "Thank you for coming with me last night. It meant such a lot to me, seeing my daughters again."

He smiled at me and nodded his head. "Yes Po-Po, I know it did. It was well worth the risk, wasn't it?"

I managed to give a little laugh. "Quite honestly Toby, being a grandmother makes me feel quite old."

His eyes sparkled. "I think there's still some life in you yet, old girl."

Well maybe there was, but I felt as if I had lived a hundred years.

THE END